What Reviewers Say About
Renee Ron͞   ͞ ͞W͞ ͞ ͞ ͞ ͞k

T0282948

Body Language

"The whole story is about self-confidence and learning to see yourself the way others—the others that matter—see you. It's about loving oneself and all aspects of oneself. I liked the body positivity message and how it translated into the sex scenes. ...The chemistry is strong, and the fact that the characters keep being surprised at how much the other wants them adds to it. I quite enjoyed reading this book, and I'll have a look at the author's other novels."
—*Jude in the Stars*

"Such a beautiful passionate story and so much more than I initially bargained for. Not only do I love the idea of this book and all the story promotes, it has a gorgeous cover that is super enticing and just made me want to pick it up without even reading the blurb, and I am so glad I did. The whole story was emotional, even if you have never been in either of the characters shoes, you can still relate, and I most certainly did. ...I loved that Renee took such an everyday, sensitive subject that we all can relate to, not matter what, and delivered an engaging and exciting story that I totally fell in love with."—*LESBIreviewed*

Where the Lies Hide

"I like the concept of the novel. The story idea is well thought out and well researched. I really connected with Cam's character..."
—*Rainbow Reflections*

"[T]his book is just what I needed. There's plenty of romantic tension, intrigue, and mystery. I wanted Sarah to find her brother as much as she did, and I struggled right alongside Cam in her discoveries."—*Kissing Backwards*

"Overall, a really great novel. Well written incredible characters, an interesting investigation storyline and the perfect amount of sexy times."—*Books, Life and Everything Nice*

"This is a fire and ice romance wrapped up in an engaging crime plot that will keep you hooked."—*Istoria Lit*

Epicurean Delights

"[*Epicurean Delights*] is captivating, with delightful humor and well-placed banter taking place between the two characters. …[T]he main characters are lovable and easily become friends we'd like to see succeed in life and in love."—*Lambda Literary Review*

"Hard Body"

"[T]he tenderness and heat make it a great read."—*reviewer@large*

"[A] short erotic story that has some beautiful emotional moments." —*Kitty Kat's Book Review Blog*

SEARCHING FOR SOMEDAY

Visit us at www.boldstrokesbooks.com

By the Author

Epicurean Delights

Stroke of Fate

Hard Body

Where the Lies Hide

Bonded Love

Body Language

Hot Days, Heated Nights

Escorted

Glass and Stone

Desires Unleashed

Decadence

Searching for Someday

SEARCHING FOR SOMEDAY

by

Renee Roman

2024

SEARCHING FOR SOMEDAY

ISBN 13: 978-1-63679-568-3

This Trade Paperback Original Is Published By
Bold Strokes Books, Inc.
P.O. Box 249
Valley Falls, NY 12185

First Edition: March 2024

CREDITS
Editor: Cindy Cresap
Production Design: Susan Ramundo
Cover Design By Jeanine Henning

Acknowledgments

It's a privilege to be able to say I am blessed by the universe.

Heartfelt thanks to Radclyffe for providing a safe place to share my craft. To Cindy Cresap, for your encouragement and guidance, and for teaching me the finer points of writing that inspire me to be the best writer I can be. Thank you, Sandy Lowe, for your honesty, feedback, and for providing a global view of the business side of writing. Jeanine Henning, you captured the heart of this story with the cover art. Thank you. And to the behind-the-scenes BSB folks, I appreciate all that you do.

A warm "thank you" to my fellow writers for the chats and cheering on. It really does help. And a special thank you to the Writing Sprints group. You are amazing, and I love you.

To the readers who spend hard-earned dollars on my books, and your kind words regarding how much you enjoyed them, my sincerest thanks. Stay tuned. There are more stories to be told, and I hope you enjoy them, too.

Engage in a meaningful life, find joy, and share your love.
Do not let these opportunities slip away.
Be brave above all else.

Namaste

CHAPTER ONE

The doorway darkened. Rayne Thomas looked up to find her mentor and principal investigator, Dr. Steven Grimes, leaning against the frame with a smile that radiated light in the windowless space.

"Hi, Dr. G. Do you need something?" Rayne took off her glasses and moved away from the microscope she'd been staring through for the last thirty minutes. Something on the slide didn't make sense, but she wasn't convinced she knew what it was. She'd jotted a few notes about what she'd seen, but it would take a bit to decipher what they meant. The word research meant just that. Searching for answers again and again.

"I read your proposal for writing a grant. The hypothesis is solid, but the experimentation is a little vague. You're going to have to dig deeper if you want my blessing."

Rayne laughed. "It's not a marriage proposal," she said as another chuckle escaped. Dr. Grimes had twenty-five-plus years in the field. If he had questions so would her funding source. "Can we meet later today to discuss it?"

"Of course. Check with Sam to find a time."

Sam, otherwise known as Samantha, was the department's administrative person, and Rayne was convinced there would be a total collapse if she left. Sam had been at the institution for more than thirty years and it would be a huge loss for the department when she retired. Rayne hoped she had moved on herself before that happened. She couldn't imagine how anyone could fill Sam's shoes.

"I'll call for an appointment as soon as I'm done here."

He shook his head. "Life was simpler at the bench than in my office." Steve quietly left.

Rayne slid her glasses in place as she turned back to the microscope. She'd only been a postdoctoral fellow for a couple of years, but she'd managed to get some interesting results during that time. Enough that she'd been able to write a paper that was published in a well-respected journal a few months ago, giving her the basis to write a research grant proposal. Rayne had wanted a career in research ever since she'd been a young girl. Living a dream didn't happen to everyone, but she'd persevered and at twenty-six, she had it all. A career she loved, a knock-out woman who adored her, and a mortgage she could afford. What more could she ask for?

❖

Sweat dripped down Maggie Flanders's neck and pooled under her breasts. It was the one part of working out she hated. She didn't mind sweating, but for some reason she'd never understood, the pooling in her sports bra grossed her out. A grunt next to her redirected her thoughts.

"Come on, Maggie, let's sprint this out." Jill, the aerobics instructor and her closest coworker, smiled as she high-stepped in a ridiculously fast rhythm.

"I thought you were my friend," she said through gritted teeth as she tried to keep pace.

"I am." Jill slowed just enough for Maggie to catch a decent breath. "That's why I push you." Jill flashed a megawatt smile at her. The one that garnered her lavish gifts from her well-off clients, the same ones who paid for private lessons.

Five minutes later, Maggie downed a bottle of room-temp water as she walked the length of the locker room. Now that the session was over, she had to admit to feeling good. The only thing that would make her feel better was a hot shower. As she gathered toiletries, her thoughts circled around to the goal she'd been cultivating the last few months. All she had to do was find a business partner willing to split responsibilities and half the cost of starting their own health and wellness center. A place where she could return to providing medical massages and strength-building workouts as well as offering meditation, tai chi, and yoga. Mind and body had to work in concert for the most benefit, and Maggie was determined to provide those much-needed services to the residents in her area. Hell, maybe someday she would have several locations. Wouldn't that be a fantastic way to reach retirement?

While the hot water streamed along her overworked muscles, Maggie wondered if a business partner was the only kind of partner in her future. She wasn't lonely, was she? A few of the women she'd dated over the last several years had been nice—necessary and diversionary—but none gave her that heart-throbbing, make her wet kind of feeling. Maybe no one ever would again. A deep melancholy settled over her making her breath catch in her chest, the pain as real as always. Ever since Eve, life had moved at its own accord and Maggie had no reason to change her ways.

CHAPTER TWO

Rayne's partner, Heather, threw a hard stare over her shoulder as they moved among the racks of summer fashions. It was foolish on her part to suggest Heather pick out more conservative outfits for work. Obviously, Heather disagreed. She had one of those perfect bodies any celebrity would pay richly for. Perfectly proportioned breasts. A flat, smooth stomach with gently flaring hips. Shapely legs. Not too tall and not too short.

How they ended up together four years ago Rayne never knew for sure, but they had. The night of tentative, erotic sex sealed her fate, and Rayne was glad it had. The whole interaction had been off the chart, not to mention the variety of things they did, and the intensity had been like nothing even her best fantasies could live up to. Heather was a sex machine. Admittedly, she was a novice in comparison but a very willing student, nonetheless.

"Honestly, Rayne, I don't know how you expect me to get ahead wearing frumpy, schoolmarm clothes." Heather pulled a very short, checked skirt off the rack and strode purposefully to a mirror. Holding it in front of her, she smiled. "This might just land me a promotion. One way or another."

She stopped sliding hangers across a long rack and tipped her head. "What does *that* mean?"

Heather laid her hand on Rayne's arm, then barely grazed her lips over her pursed ones. "Oh, nothing." She laughed. "I was joking! Gee!" Plucking a few more questionable items from nearby racks, she turned over-bright eyes at her. "I'm going to try these on. Why don't you go look for something over there." She pointed in the area of the middle-aged, sophisticated section and smirked.

"Heather, I really don't..." When Rayne turned back around, Heather was standing in front of the mirror ogling her own reflection before sashaying into a fitting room. Silently sighing, she headed over to another section called *Smart Woman*. It was the area of the store designated for the not-quite-fat clientele. She'd gained a few pounds over the last year or so. Being in the lab or sitting at a computer for twelve hours a day didn't help, but she still had a decent shape, even if it wasn't the shape it once was. Heather had mentioned the spread of her ass more than once, and Rayne did her best in the battle to maintain a size fourteen. She was curvy and she happened to like her curves.

Annoyed by the whole subject, she pulled a couple of items from the limited selections and threw them over her arm, knowing she might as well keep herself occupied. Heather could try on clothes for hours and end up buying a select few, if any at all. They had to be "perfect," like her.

❖

Later that night following an afternoon in bed, Rayne pushed unappetizing food around her plate as Heather gorged herself on fettuccine alfredo with chicken until Rayne found the nerve to ask something that had been on her mind since the beginning. "What about me made you ask me to dance the night we met?"

The fork stopped mid-twirl, Heather's eyes narrowing. "Why are you asking now?"

Rayne shrugged. "Sometimes I get the feeling you're making do...being with me, and I want to know what you saw in me, then... and now." She swallowed around the lump in her throat. Taking chances at work and trying things that she thought might end with positive results was one thing, but taking a chance with Heather had been a big "what if" and the unease she was feeling needed quieting.

Heather looked uncomfortable as she set her fork down and stared at her plate. When she did look up, she smiled too big before saying anything. "You were fun, and it wasn't long before I found out you're willing to try just about anything." She raised her eyebrows several times, then picked up her fork and started eating again.

"And now?"

Heather glanced up through her eyelashes, then followed with another sentence in the way she'd come to know so well. "Being with you makes me feel good about myself."

And there it was. The self-centered statements that Rayne had begun to hear more and more of. If she were a betting woman, she'd double down that Heather's comment was a thinly veiled insult. It should have devastated her or at the very least, made her angry, but she stayed silent for a long time. She should have questioned her further, somehow feeling like Heather had avoided the real questions. Rayne didn't want to push her and make her mad after the earth-shattering orgasms she'd had when they got home and, honestly, she wanted more in the future.

❖

Six months later, Rayne finally found the courage to confront Heather about her constant "overtime." She came breezing through the door at midnight, kicked off her heels, and tossed her coat on a nearby chair. The slinky green dress she wore was low-cut and form-fitting. It clung to her curves like it was painted on. If that's what she was wearing to work, Rayne could only imagine what kind of work Heather was doing. She watched from a dark corner of the living room as Heather hummed a sultry tune and headed for the kitchen, totally unaware of her presence as she strode by and groaned.

"God, I'm starving."

Rayne stood as Heather opened the refrigerator. When she closed it again and turned with a leftover sub in one hand and a bottle of wine in the other, Rayne flicked on the light, startling her.

"Shit!" she cried out, then laughed nervously. "You scared me half to death! What are you doing lurking around in the dark?"

Completely ignoring her, she clenched her fists against her thighs and spoke through gritted teeth. "Did you work up an appetite tonight?"

Heather set her items down before making eye contact. "Uh, yeah. We had this deadline to meet and there just wasn't any time to…" She noticeably swallowed before she continued. "What's that look for?"

Rayne felt the heat rise in her face. "Do you take me for a complete idiot? I know damned well you weren't working wearing that." She pointed at the dress for emphasis. "So where were you?"

Her face became hard as stone as she pressed her palms on the surface of the breakfast bar. "I told you. I was working." Her eyes bored into Rayne's. It was obvious she was waiting for her to acquiesce as she'd always done in the past. This time was going to be different. For both of them.

"I called your office. I called your cell phone."

Heather let out a breath and smiled too sweetly at her. "I wasn't in my office, silly. I was with the boss. I haven't even looked at my phone and it was on silent." She grabbed a glass and poured some wine, then took a deep drink. "Sorry I missed your calls."

"Liar."

Her eyes grew wide in shock before they morphed into a cold stare. Rayne couldn't bear to look at her any longer. As she turned away, she heard her hiss. That's when the ranting began.

"What the fuck did you expect me to do? You've turned into a cow, and I'm embarrassed to have you around me. I needed to find someone I could take to company functions and be proud they were with me."

Rayne snapped her head around, shocked at the hurtful things Heather had said.

Pain and anguish must have registered on her face because Heather attempted to justify herself. "Oh, come on, Rayne. You know it's true. You've gotten lazy and you don't care what you look like anymore. Don't try to blame that on *me*."

"Why would you say such awful things? What have I done to deserve this? Cheating on me. Calling me names?" She couldn't stop the tears once they began. She wasn't sure what she expected at that point, but it sure as hell wasn't what came out of Heather's mouth next.

"It doesn't matter now. You've been replaced." Heather refilled her glass and grabbed her food as she headed for the couch. She flicked on the TV and began to tear into the submarine, acting as though she hadn't just ripped Rayne's world apart.

She wasn't aware of how long she stood there, too shocked to move, unable to say anything. After Heather was done, she gathered the remnants of her meal and took them to the kitchen. Watching her in disbelief, Rayne slumped into a chair.

Heather leaned down and whispered in her ear on her way past. "You know, you had it made, until you forgot who you were with. You've lost me, but then, I knew it wasn't gonna last. You were never good enough for me."

CHAPTER THREE

"M rs. Johnson, how about if you try this way?" Maggie adjusted the woman's grip on the elliptical, which in turn helped her rhythm.

"It's Claudia," she gasped. After a few more times, she shared a tentative, but grateful smile. "That's so much better, Maggie."

Maggie smiled. She loved helping those who were struggling, especially when it came to their confidence level. The water bottle in the holder was nearly empty, and she took it to the water cooler. When she returned, Maggie checked the heart rate reading on the display. Claudia was well within a safe range. "Looking good. Keep it up for another ten, then slow down easy."

"I remember."

One of the first times Claudia had used the treadmill, she'd abruptly stopped and tried to step off right away. Lucky for her, there were several people milling around who caught her in time to avoid a nasty fall. She wasn't there to badger clients, but giving a friendly reminder every so often was a good policy she didn't forget to practice. She made the rounds while she waited for her next tabata class of mixed-age participants. The thirty-minute routine she'd developed would push some and make others wish it was a little longer, but that was the goal of the gym, to make all the activities enjoyable. Well, as enjoyable as possible for everyone.

It was one of the reasons she'd joined five years ago. Little did she know then that the owner had been watching her for weeks before offering her a full-time position, saying she had a natural talent. It wasn't a hard decision. Doing massages was great, but the numbers were unpredictable, and Maggie had bills to pay. She still had several regular customers who depended on her for monthly massages, plus she liked the extra income and rarely turned anyone down.

"Hey, Maggie." Jill crossed the space to the registration desk in long strides. She was taller than Maggie by several inches and leaner.

"I thought you were off today?"

"Yeah." Jill laughed. "So did I until Mark called in with a stomach bug." She hung her jacket on a hook behind the desk. "It's not like I can't use the hours." Jill had two children she was raising on her own. The youngest was in fifth grade and her son was starting high school in the fall. He was growing like a weed, and Jill had a hard time keeping food in the house and clothes on his back. "You have a class starting soon, don't you?"

Maggie checked one of the big clocks randomly placed around the facility. People needed to know the time when they worked out, unlike casinos who were happy their customers lost track of time and gambled longer than they might have if they knew how long they'd been there. "Fifteen minutes till tabata." She grabbed her refillable bottle and went to the nearest cooler. "Too bad you can't join in on the fun."

"If you're looking to pay me back for the aerobics class, you can forget it. I'm not letting you pound me into the pavement." Jill grinned knowingly. It was a healthy competition between them to see who could beat the other. Mostly they finished the workouts by sheer will, neither willing to quit until the last exercise was completed.

She put her hand to her heart. "Ouch. Would I do that to you?"

"Yes. In a heartbeat." Jill winked. "Same as I would."

"That's not—"

"Hi, Maggie." Lindsay, a nineteen-year-old college freshman, ran up to Maggie. The crush she did nothing to hide was a little annoying, but harmless. "You're teaching the class, right?" Hope was apparent in the lilt of her voice.

"Hey, Lindsay. It starts in ten minutes. Why don't you go warm up and I'll be there in a minute."

"Sure." Lindsay practically skipped to the second room on the right.

"Oh, she's got it bad for you." Jill hip-bumped her. "It's kinda cute."

"It's annoying, but bearable, and the main reason I never go in a room with her until there's more people." The last thing she needed was a scandal in the gym. Bad enough the older women made sure she knew they were interested by signing up for all the one-on-one training sessions they could get in on. She'd seen a couple of them outside of the gym, but she made sure they knew her rules up front. No long-term relationships, and if she slept with someone, it was for a limited time. No exceptions. Life was much simpler that way, and simple was good.

❖

Maggie stepped out of the shower and considered taking an over-the-counter medication. She was sore from the three classes she'd taught today and there were two more on the schedule for tomorrow. Maybe she could talk Larry into taking one for her. Her phone buzzed and she glanced at the screen in time to see it was her mother.

It had been almost a week since they'd talked, and she missed their easy conversation. She glanced at the digital clock. The time of her call was a little disconcerting and she swiped the screen before it went dark, then pressed the speaker button.

"Hey, Mom. Is everything alright?" Not one to spread panic, she kept the worry out of her voice.

"Hi, dear. Everything is fine. I've been a social butterfly lately and needed to hear my daughter's voice. I hope I haven't caught you at a bad time."

Maggie let out the breath she'd been holding and squirted lotion in her hand. Her mother would be proud. She'd been adamant about self-care when Maggie was young, and she'd never forgotten the lessons. "It's never a bad time to have a chat with my mom. What's going on in the old neighborhood?"

Her mother sighed. "Sometimes I wish there was a reason it was a bad time, in a good way."

"Mom, I told you, I'm not interested in another relationship. I'm fine with being single." She told her mother the same thing she told herself every time she saw a couple who acted like they were securely in love.

"Being fine isn't the same as being happy. You're a wonderful person and you deserve to *be* happy with someone who loves you. Don't you think it's time, baby girl?"

Her mother's use of her childhood term of endearment was a sure sign she was worried. She thought about Jill and the sparkle in her eyes when she talked about her children. Then the smile that formed when Larry relayed a story about an event he and his girlfriend attended, and she knew his smile had nothing to do with where they went or what they did; it was because he was thinking about his partner. Would she even remember how to enjoy moments like that, or would the shadow of the past eclipse the light of the present?

"Maggie, you there?"

She jolted back to the present. "I'm here. I'll think about it, Mom, okay?"

Her mother managed to mostly hide the deep sigh she heard from the other end. "I don't mean to nag, but you deserve it, baby girl."

"Thanks, Mom. Now tell me all about the shenanigans at home. Has Dad been behaving or is he still Jonesing for that expensive sports car?"

Her mom laughed and dove in with a detailed list of her father's latest gimmicks, pranks, and whining about not getting his way, though they both knew he'd get whatever he wanted in the end. Just like the entire Flanders clan. She missed their conversations. Mostly, she missed coming home and talking about her day with someone other than Draper, the tuxedo cat she couldn't resist adopting a few years ago. Before she hung up, she promised to call the following week and make plans to visit.

"Meow."

She felt Draper's velvet fur against her bare leg after announcing he was none too pleased at having his dinner delayed. Maggie had fixed herself some food while she talked with her mom, and she was just about to settle down with a beer in front of the TV and scroll through the streaming networks in hopes of landing on something fun to zone out on.

"You do know I'm not your servant, right?"

"Meow."

Maggie snatched him from the floor and rubbed her face in his luxurious coat. Whenever she did that, the world didn't seem so aloof. Not like Draper at times when all he was interested in was his dish. She just happened to be the means to an end, and she swore he used it to his advantage. "Why do I spoil you, you ungrateful pest?"

"Meow." Draper looked at her with that coquettish gleam in his eyes that let her know she'd already lost the battle of wills.

When she put him down, he went and sat next to his dish and all she could do was laugh. He had her tightly wrapped around his paw and they both knew it. She didn't want any human relationship to resemble that kind of tight control, but a firm stroke to her ego now and again wouldn't be so bad.

After she shook some of the moist food into Draper's extra dish and set it down, he began to purr in earnest. Ah, to live the simple existence of a well-cared-for cat. She gave his back a long stroke. "Since my services are no longer needed, Dray, I'm going to have that beer now and veg. Feel free to join me." Maggie shook her head and dropped on the end of the couch, her legs extended on the lounge end. The bottle met her lips, and she took a few short draws, resisting the temptation to empty it. The words from her mother sank deeper and found purchase in the corner of her brain where she stored her pain and the memories that accompanied them.

She wondered if her destiny was to spend her evenings with a creature who often acted as though she was an entity who had to be tolerated for their own comforts. That wasn't how she wanted to live her life. The problem was, she wasn't sure what she wanted and there was no crystal ball to show her the way. Until that changed, she'd continue doing what she did. In solitude.

CHAPTER FOUR

The lights in the house were low and the room held a chill as Rayne shuffled through the eerily quiet house. She tried to swallow before remembering it had been hours since she drank anything. Even longer since she'd eaten.

"Fuck."

She ran her fingers through her unwashed, tangled hair and stared out the kitchen window. The process of thinking was tiresome, which was ironic since she was a scientist. Thinking was what she did. It was past time she got back to it. To her life. To her work. She'd once again let Heather's influence run her life, but she wasn't about to let her *ruin* it, too.

Squinting as the kitchen light flared, Rayne bent to look in the fridge. The contents were paltry and scary at best. An egg carton that might have two edible eggs. A wilted head of romaine. A carton of milk that she couldn't remember buying. A Chinese take-out container she vaguely recalled bringing home more than a week ago. A can of flavored seltzer. As the only viable offering that wouldn't give her food poisoning, she popped open the seltzer and downed half the contents. It was pretty flat, but wet and cold was good enough. Her pitiful state sank in further as she caught her reflection in the small mirror hanging next to the back door.

Her once carefully coiffed hair stuck up in a thousand directions, probably due to the amount of grease covering the strands. She wasn't one of those people who could get away with not washing it for a day or two. Her face was smudged with God knows what, the visible tear tracks were the only clean areas. The clothes she wore weren't any cleaner. Evidence of whatever her last meal was stained the front of her shirt. As she lifted the can to her lips once more, she glimpsed her fingernails and retched.

How the fuck did I get here? Wherever the fuck here was.

Rayne drained the rest of the can, tossed it, and let out a shout of victory when it landed in the trash can. The contents of the fridge found the same home. The next destination was the bathroom. She didn't bother to stop for clothes. She didn't want to touch anything until she'd scrubbed away the grime of however many days. Had it been a week since she showered? A hard shiver ran down her spine. She'd called out sick the Monday after Heather left claiming she had the flu. She tried to figure out what day it was before shrugging. It didn't matter. She desperately needed a shower.

The hot water streaming over her felt like a baptism of sorts. A washing away of all the inertia and self-doubt that had accumulated in her brain. Her breaths came easier. They were the first real ones she'd taken in months. The idea that she'd been waiting for the wheels to fall off the relationship bus for a while was a hard pill to swallow, and hot tears fell as she soaped the sponge. Though she'd been devastated, then sad, after Heather's departure, she knew deep down Heather had been involved with someone else for a while. But then to go on to blame Rayne for the reason she'd been seeing another, that had been the greatest insult, surpassed only by calling her a cow. A fucking cow. As the last of the tears mingled with the grime flowing down the drain, Rayne was caught in memories of the not-so-distant past.

That night she waited up for Heather to confront her was the start of the end. A week later, Heather was gone. When she left, Rayne burned sage, making sure it was everywhere, just like Heather's lingering scent was everywhere. She wasn't about to give up her home. There'd be other people who would come and go in her life. She couldn't very well move every time that happened, unless it was for a position she couldn't pass up.

She glanced up and narrowed her gaze at the woman staring back. At least she was recognizable. And clean. Rayne tipped her head. There was a noise in her bedroom. She took off at a sprint. The prospect of hearing a human voice made her lightheaded. She'd turned the sound off on her phone at some point and now it was vibrating along her dresser.

"Hello?" Her voice was a little breathy and a lot needy, but she didn't care.

"Rayne? It's Steve." A pause followed. "Are you alright?"

"I...I wasn't doing well for a few days, Dr. Grimes. I'm better today." She switched screens. What would he think if she didn't even know what day it was. Thursday. She'd lost three days during her mental absence. Jesus. "I can come in and catch up." It was the last thing she wanted, but he'd always been fair and understanding. The least she could do was go to the lab for a few hours and see where things were, pick up the pieces.

"You'll do no such thing."

"But my paper—"

"Will wait." Dr. Grimes's voice was firm. "Rayne, you were a dedicated student and now you're a dedicated scientist. I know you wouldn't have called out if you didn't need to." His tone had softened. "Take the rest of the week and come back Monday. We'll recap where you are and your plans for the next month. How does that sound?"

Gratitude flooded her senses. When it came time to decide whether to accept Dr. Grimes's offer for a postdoctoral fellow position in his lab, move to another lab to expand her experience and learn new techniques, or to leave the institution altogether Rayne had to weigh what would be best for her career. In the end, her heart was set on continuing the work she'd begun with her thesis. She'd gotten little to no support from Heather in her career goals. That should have resulted in a glaring red flag a while ago, but she was enamored by the sexy way Heather did most things. A swing of her hips, biting her lip, and the screams that ensued when she orgasmed. A valuable lesson was learned in the wake. A relationship at this point in her career was never going to work, especially if it sucked the life out of her.

Now she had a chance to focus her attention on where it belonged. She wanted to see it through, push the boundaries of what was known and what she might possibly be able to discover by expanding the scope of her research. There was no doubt she'd made the right choice.

"Thank you. I really appreciate the extra time, Dr. Grimes."

"You're welcome, Rayne, and please, it's Steve. We're colleagues with the same degree."

Addressing superiors in any way other than formally had always been difficult. "I'll do my best, Steve." She couldn't help smiling while they ended the call, and warmth spread through her knowing he cared about her as a person, not just a body in the lab.

She dropped the towel and turned to the full-length mirror, staring at the pale reflection. Her breasts were nicely shaped. Full, but not droopy. Rayne's gaze moved downward to the slight bulge of her stomach. It had never been flat, even as a child she had a little rise in her lower belly. She found it sexy on femmes though she wasn't attracted to femmes. Huh. Heather was a high femme, so what had it been about her that Rayne couldn't resist? Was it more that she'd been enamored by the attention, rather than the person? Was Heather a femme or a femme fatale? Was Rayne destined to be drawn in by predators only to be cast off when she no longer provided a meal?

Rayne laughed out loud as she ran her hand down her center. Who was she kidding? The reason she'd pursued Heather wasn't her looks, or how she presented. Plain and simple, it had been the sex. Sex with Heather had been mind-blowing. The best Rayne had ever had.

"Oh well. It was good while it lasted," she said to her reflection.

She dried her hair, put on comfortable clothes, and gathered her things. Rayne pulled her shoulders back, opened the door, and stepped into her future. She was a scientist. Someday she might find what she was searching for. Not a scientific result, but a human one.

The plate was empty save for some crumbs. Rayne was too self-conscious to lick them up. She'd feasted on a chicken Caesar salad wrap and a bowl of minestrone soup, savoring every morsel. Normally a coffee hound, Rayne had opted for an unsweetened decaf iced tea with lemon. Since she was unsure if her stomach could handle the caffeine, the tea was a better choice. Fully sated, she relaxed against the padded booth and pulled out paper and a pen. Next up was a trip to the grocer, and she needed to make a list of staple foods and other necessities missing from her house. When she was in self-imposed quarantine and ran out of whatever it was, she shrugged it off and went without. Even now she wasn't sure if there was a supply of toilet tissue.

The waitress arrived a few minutes later with her check and refreshed her iced tea. She smiled and thanked her before draining the glass, then she left an enormous tip. After a quick stop in the restroom, she was ready to face the rest of her day. For the first time in what felt like forever, she was happy. Rayne hadn't realized how much control Heather had over her psyche. Rather, that she let her control it. If she was going to start being honest about her situation, it was time she stopped trying to kid herself. There was a time when she was perfectly content to just exist in the fantasy world that was all Heather's making. That little scene was over and done with though, and there was no way in hell history was going to repeat itself.

A few hours later, the refrigerator stocked, and her laundry done, Rayne sat down with her phone, pressed a button, and waited impatiently while the monotone woman told her she had three missed calls. The first was her dentist's office, reminding her of her appointment for a cleaning she'd missed two days ago. *Shit.* The second was the receptionist confirming the missed cleaning and could she please call at her first convenience to reschedule. Double shit. She hated missing appointments.

Next up was the dreaded clothing issue. She stood in the doorway, shocked at what she saw. Her "half" of the closet had been reduced to a third, maybe less, with most of the long poles that spanned the sides, empty. How had she not noticed? She shook her head, something that had happened a lot over the last week. This was another reminder how little she'd paid attention to her day-to-day life, or cared about herself in the last—how long—six months? Maybe a year? How pathetic to have let things get so far.

While she rummaged, groaned, and tossed item after item, one thing became clear. Heather was right about her not caring how she looked. So far she'd made four piles of clothes. The dry-cleaning pile had a few items that Rayne didn't dare attempt to wash. Another stack needed pretreating for stains that would take a nuclear explosion to remove, but she was going to try anyway, even if she had to wash them twice because they were favorites. A third pile held articles of clothing that were just plain horrible, and she wasn't even sure if they were hers because they fit so poorly. Those were designated for the clothing donation drop box. The final pile didn't look half bad. She went to repeat the process with the dresser. The top two drawers were bare except for some discarded packaging and stockings with holes. Why the hell had she been relegated to the bottom drawers? *Because you allowed it.* That voice that popped into her head was annoying as hell. It was time she shut it down.

Chapter Five

From where she stood, Maggie had a clear view of the equipment, weight machines, and the open, matted area where clients stretched and performed exercises. Most had been coming to the gym for a while, but there were a few who were new. The guy on the elliptical worked at a nice pace and seemed comfortable and relaxed. Clearly, this wasn't his first time in a gym, so she moved her gaze on to the next person. Another man, slightly older and softer. His form was average and his stride slow. Maybe he'd been a mall walker and decided he needed something different. A couple of machines to the left, there was a woman who'd caught her attention from a few days ago. She appeared tentative and unsure. She didn't make eye contact either. Maggie got the impression she was shy rather than snobbish. In the next few days, she'd introduce herself and offer a friendly face. Working out was hard enough; having a familiar face might help put her at ease. She rested her forearm on the counter and leaned toward Larry.

"Hey."

Larry glanced away from the computer. "Hey yourself." He smiled.

"Do you know the woman in the white top and blue shorts? I don't think I've seen her before." She tipped her head slightly in the woman's direction.

"Hmm." Larry tapped on the keyboard a few times. "I think her name is Rayne."

Maggie snapped head around. "Rayne?" She sideways glanced at the dark-haired woman again. "You sure?"

"Here." Larry swung the screen around. A driver's license image filled the screen, the image unmistakable, along with the name, Rayne Thomas. He turned the screen back. "You tailing her?" That was Larry's way of asking about her interest level.

"No." She wasn't quite there. "I thought I'd be friendly and introduce myself. It looks like she's struggling a bit. Maybe a few encouraging words would cheer her up."

Larry guffawed. "I'm not sure someone with a body like yours should be trying to cheer anyone in here up."

Maggie's eyebrows knit as her eyes narrowed. "What the hell does that mean?"

"Come on, Maggie. You're a female version of Atlas and you know it. You never flaunt it, but your physique makes everyone here feel like that puny guy on the beach." Larry didn't sound mad, more like he was just stating facts.

She'd worked hard for how she was, on the inside and out. Maggie had been that puny gal on the beach. Pale, rail thin, and weak. She didn't have any delusions about not being attractive, but she had a decent six-pack and biceps that were proof she'd put in the work to escape the childhood ridicule of being someone the other kids could bully. Maybe Larry had a point.

"I'm sorry you feel that way. I'm not here to make anyone feel bad about who they are or what they look like." It wasn't her responsibility to change people's idea of envy. "I did this for me. There's a lot of emotional trauma behind how people see me, and I did this to prove to myself there's all kinds of ways to heal. This was mine." All the years of teasing and ridicule up to when she entered college had made her who she was. She'd secretly worked out in high school, then went full on in college while she earned her degree and fell in love. When Eve died, she'd lost parts of herself and the only glue that kept her from falling apart was the gym.

"I didn't know." Larry rested his hand on her forearm and the muscles beneath his touch rippled.

"Most people don't." She glanced at Rayne, sweat dripping down her face. She turned to Larry again. "All you had to do was ask." She slid her arm away and went to the weight machine for the ten-minute lift that would settle her.

❖

"Larry and I are going for a beer. Want to join us?" Jill made an entry into one of the computers.

A wave of anxiety coursed through Maggie before she glanced up to see Larry making a hands heart and looking innocent. She couldn't help but laugh. She was fortunate to work with good people, even if at times they didn't really know her, but that was true for most people, and she wasn't about to hold a grudge.

"Who's buying?"

Jill clapped her shoulder. "I'll get the first round if you're in."

Yeah, she could definitely do worse. "Deal."

They finished closing up and walked the two blocks to the bar. Pete's Pub, formerly known as For Pete's Sake, was a local favorite. When she first started working at Fitness with Finesse, Jill had taken her there to welcome her to the neighborhood. Since then, she dropped in once a week for a drink and food, as much to do her part in supporting local businesses as to enjoy the homey atmosphere. It was like she belonged to something larger than her own circle of comfort.

Once settled into a large booth with extra leg room, which they appreciated, they ordered drinks and perused the well-known menu. Not because they needed it, but because it was always hard to choose what to have.

"So, have you introduced yourself to Rayne?" Larry hadn't mentioned their little disagreement from a few days ago until now.

"I haven't seen her."

Jill glanced between them, a quizzical look on her face. "What are you two up to?"

Maggie dropped her menu, knowing what she wanted to eat. "There's a couple of new clients that I haven't worked with yet."

"And this woman is one you want to?" Jill's eyebrow rose.

She hated that her "player" status had followed her to the gym, but she was adamant about no long-term relationships, so it was bound to happen. In her own defense, she rarely acted on any attraction she had for a client. She knew the policy and she was careful with how she interacted with customers at work. On the rare occasion when the interest was reciprocal, she made sure it took place outside of the gym, making it clear that business was business, and there'd be no favoritism inside the walls where she worked.

"Maggie?"

"Huh?"

"What's your plan?" Jill gazed at her, a question in her eyes.

"Chicken Caesar wrap and fries?" She looked from Jill to Larry and back again.

"She's asking about Rayne," Larry said.

The world shrank and her vision filled with all the women she had any sort of interaction with. Maggie faced Jill. "I'm going to talk to her. Introduce myself and help her if I can."

Jill studied her for what seemed like a very long time. "You're good like that. I'm sure she'd appreciate it." Jill picked up her menu. "I'm having the bacon blue burger and onion rings."

Apparently, the subject was closed, and Maggie was happy to not be the topic of conversation. The waitress placed their drinks on the table, and they ordered food. Larry got wings and a personal pizza. He might not have the biggest muscles, but he certainly had a huge appetite. She'd bet money he would eat everything he ordered and whatever was left on their plates.

CHAPTER SIX

The treadmill slowed to a near stop and Rayne stepped off, then promptly took a header. She was struggling to recover when the sultry trainer with the sculptured body came to her rescue. When Rayne was back on her feet, the trainer held her at arm's length and shared a gentle smile.

"Does anything hurt?"

Her insides twisted uncomfortably. "Just my pride."

The trainer glanced at the offending piece of equipment. "Don't worry about it. You'd be surprised how often that happens," the trainer said reassuringly. Her eyes roved over Rayne's body and heat traveled to her face. "It looks like you're going to live to see another workout." She stuck her hand out. "I'm Maggie, one of the personal trainers."

Tentatively grasping her outstretched hand confirmed her strength in the simple touch. It wasn't painful but was firm enough that there was no doubt Maggie was into more than just treadmills. "Rayne. Thank you for the hand up." She shook it once before attempting to let go. Beautiful women made her nervous. Hot ones even more so. Maggie wasn't so quick to break contact.

"Are you sure you're all right?" Genuine concern laced her words and Rayne sank into them for a moment. It had been a while since a woman had cared about what happened to her. Heather never asked how she was.

"I'm fine. Bruised ego is all." The warmth in her cheeks remained.

"Great name by the way. You're new to Fitness. Welcome. Is this your first time here?"

"Umm, I think it's my fourth."

It must have become obvious that Rayne was struggling to regain composure because Maggie slowly released her hand and moved it reassuringly to her shoulder. "Everyone starts somewhere. How about I show you how to use some of the equipment?"

"Sure." Rayne nodded in agreement, more to get away from the humiliation corner she was in rather than any real desire to find out how to torture her body. Forty minutes later, she had enough knowledge to keep from seriously injuring herself. She was grateful for Maggie's patience and kind understanding. They were standing at one of the benches while she drank some much-needed water, when Maggie began asking questions.

"So, Rayne, what's your goal?"

Feeling more at ease, she thought for a couple moments. "I need to lose some weight and tone up." Rayne finished her water, her mood switching from light to serious.

Maggie appeared genuinely interested. "You need?" She made a face like she had a bad taste in her mouth. "You don't *need* to do anything, Rayne, unless that's what you really want."

"I'll never be model material. That's okay. I've no desire to spend the majority of my free time at the gym, but I'd like to drop a size or two and then decide if I want more."

One side of Maggie's face lifted in a wry smile. "You're the first person in a long line who didn't come in saying that wanted to be a ten. It's refreshing."

"Thanks." She wondered if there was a hidden meaning. "I think."

She stroked her full lower lip with her thumb and Rayne's pulse sped up. Between that and Maggie's glistening, tan skin, she was going to need to sit down if she didn't get away soon. "How does my promise to help you reach your goals if you promise to give me three months to get you there sound?"

Three months. It had taken her more than a year to gain the extra weight she now carried. Her curiosity was piqued. "What's my end of the bargain?"

Laughing, Maggie gestured to a nearby bench. "You come five days a week, two hours a day for the first month. After that, I'll let you know. If you're serious about being fit, I can help. If not, let me know at that point and I can save you some money."

Confusion set in. She was coming to the gym whether Maggie trained her or not. There must have been something telling on her face because Maggie picked up the conversation.

"Personal trainers aren't included in your membership. To have me all to yourself will cost you thirty dollars a session."

Rayne frowned. A hundred and fifty bucks a week was a lot of money for someone existing on a single income. She made decent money as a researcher, but with a mortgage and a car payment, she wasn't sure she could swing it.

Maggie went to the counter and grabbed a business card. She wrote something on the back and brought it over. "You don't have to decide tonight. Not everyone can afford a PT. Take a few days to consider it. If you say yes, I guarantee you'll like the results."

She arched a brow. "Guarantee, huh?"

"Oh, yeah." Maggie leaned close and her musky scent wafted around her buzzing head. Maggie's smile was infectious.

Rayne smiled back. "I'll think about it."

Maggie tapped the card in her hand. "My cell number is on the back. Call me anytime to ask questions or give me your decision. Either way, I'm glad you've turned your attention on you. A lot of people forget to do that. I'll help you however I can." She grabbed a fresh towel and headed in the direction of a client whose shirt was caught in a piece of equipment.

She called out to her, not wanting to sever the singularly focused connection they'd shared for a little while. "Thanks, Maggie."

"Sure. Anytime."

When Rayne turned, several blondes had their heads together, giggling while looking right at her. If it weren't for Maggie, embarrassment might have kept her from coming back to the gym. Her offer might not be a cut-rate discount, but it was worth considering. Especially since she seemed enthusiastic about her off to help. As the women continued to snicker in the background, she hung on to the idea that Maggie had approached *her*. Maggie asked to be *her* trainer. The women could make all the noise they wanted, but Rayne was the one who would be close and personal with Maggie for ten hours a week. Maybe if she forced herself to get over the nervousness of being around someone with a body like Maggie's she'd find the confidence she needed to not only survive her personal life, but to also succeed in the world of science. All she had to do was figure out what she could sacrifice in her budget to pull it off. Totally worth it.

❖

"You've got this. Just two more minutes. Push." Maggie was a great cheerleader, but Rayne's legs were rubber and two more minutes might end up with her on the floor. The treadmill wasn't necessarily her enemy, however, with a nine percent incline, they were going to have words. As soon as she could breathe without gasping.

"Done!" Maggie's enthusiasm was exuberant.

Rayne struggled to stay upright as she lowered the machine's speed, giving her legs time to recover a bit.

Maggie hit the stop button after Rayne moved her feet off the tread. "That was great, Rayne. You're doing fantastic." Maggie gave her a towel. "Drink the rest of your water, then shake out your legs so you don't cramp."

With her breathing a little more settled, she finished the water and did as directed.

"How are you feeling?" Maggie asked.

When was the last time anyone asked her that? Her parents? Her guidance counselor? Never Heather. Not once. What did that reveal about their relationship? Had they even had a relationship? And here was an almost stranger who at least appeared to care. So how did she feel? "I'm good." It was true. The work was hard, and Maggie was a taskmaster, but she was also aware of the edge of Rayne's limits and pushed her just enough that she could feel her body changing and getting stronger. "Thanks for today."

"You're welcome, but you did all the work." Maggie smiled and went to the desk.

Once she cooled down, she headed to the shower. Twenty minutes later and no longer feeling like the walking dead, Rayne strode through the gym on light feet. She was physically tired but mentally elated. She'd run longer than she thought possible, lifted weights, and completed a circuit. Outside, she paused to inhale the cool night air. With her eyes closed, Rayne took stock of her elevated mood. Her research was going well, and she was almost ready to submit a grant proposal. Steve wanted to meet with her to discuss tweaks and suggestions, but since she would be the principal investigator if she was awarded research money, he would leave the final decision on changes to her. A deep voice startled her.

"Enjoying the last of the sun?" Maggie carried a large gym bag that didn't seem to weigh her down in the least. She wore a pair of ripped jeans and a button-down spring green shirt that highlighted her gray-green eyes. The street clothes semi-hid the toned body beneath. She didn't have to use her imagination for most of what lay beneath because Maggie wore a sports bra and spandex shorts when she worked, showing off the definition of her muscle. And she had a lot of them.

"It's such a nice evening." Rayne stole a glance. She shouldn't be looking at her trainer like she was fangirling.

"That it is." Maggie hesitated, something she never did in the gym. She faced Rayne. "I'm grabbing a bite to eat. Would you like to join me?"

Her heart skipped one beat, then another as she tried to make sense of what was happening. Was Maggie asking her to go on a date? That would be wishful thinking on her part, and she almost laughed out loud at the absurdity. Why the hell would Maggie be interested in her? Sure, she was on a journey and Maggie was there to help, but it wasn't personal, it was professional. While her hopes included becoming a more confident version of herself and gaining solid ground after several weeks of fretting about what she had to offer in a relationship, Rayne needed to stop the negativity. She was smart, sometimes funny. She was sexy. Well, at least she had believed that was true at one point in her life. That was around the same time Heather breezed into her life. Heather was gone and so was her certainty about her attributes. She definitely wasn't ready to date. She might never be self-assured enough for the likes of Maggie. Her silence must have indicated to Maggie that she didn't think it was a good idea.

"I'm sorry. No pressure, Rayne." Her gaze lowered. "Have a good night." Maggie turned away.

Her pulse raced. "Maggie?"

"Yes?" Maggie took a step closer.

"Can we walk to the restaurant? I need a little more of a stretch." The smile that formed on Maggie's face made her lightheaded.

"Three blocks in that direction." Maggie pointed down the street where people strolled and talked.

Her gaze followed where Maggie indicated. No one appeared in a hurry, and neither was she. "Do they have wine?"

"Absolutely."

Mistake or not, this felt right, and Rayne was going with it.

CHAPTER SEVEN

"Hi, Dad. How have you been?" Maggie talked louder to be heard over the sound of the TV blaring in the background. "Hey, Mag, it's good to hear your voice." The TV volume disappeared. "I'm doing as well as an old coot can expect." He laughed at his own joke. Her father was on the young side of old. "How's life at the gym?"

"It's good."

"Still looking for a business partner?" her father asked. She'd shared the idea with him six months ago and it was a frequent topic. He offered to be a silent partner, but Maggie was determined to set up the business on her own.

"Yeah. Not that many people are interested in taking a chance with their life savings. I'm lucky that you and Mom provided me the opportunity to decide where my passion was through trial and error." A lump formed in her throat. Neither working at a gym nor wanting to own a business had been on her radar before she started college. She let her original dream go to embrace new ones. That had to count for something. "Thanks, Dad."

Her father let out a sigh. "Maggie, you're my daughter. Your mom and I have experienced trying to find that perfect niche where you just know in your bones what you're supposed to do. It takes time, girl. We're happy we could give that to our children."

Maggie smiled because he meant every word. "So am I, Dad." She fiddled with a Fitness by Finesse business card. Except for the number she'd printed on the back, it was just like the one she'd given to Rayne. Before melancholy could grab ahold, she changed the subject. "Speaking of trying things, any idea where that wandering brother of mine is these days?" They both laughed for a bit. No one in the family quite grasped Jason's desire to chase storms across the world and live out of an oversized duffel bag. He had no home except for the one their parents owned, and it was the only place he had ever needed. He was content to travel the continents to learn what real climate change looked like up close. Jason took every opportunity to speak with the people who somehow managed to survive the unpredictable weather that impacted their lives. She had to give him credit. He lived simply and worked hard. Jason didn't lie awake at night stewing over meaningless worries and the material things that at the end of the day, didn't hold any value. Maggie pictured her father with his head tipped and his eyes narrowed as he thought.

"Somewhere in the tropics chasing hurricanes. Why that boy insists on taking chances like that, I'll never know." The worry in his voice was hard to miss, and the love that ran beneath it was loud and clear.

"He's a man, not a boy, Dad. Besides, he loves what he does, even if the rest of the family doesn't understand it." Why did anyone do what they did? "All we have to do is love and support him."

Her father sighed through the phone. "I know you're right, honey. As a parent, the worrying never stops."

Did that mean he worried about her, too? Granted, she wasn't globetrotting and in danger of Mother Nature's wrath, but there were other kinds of worry, and her parents were aware she hadn't loved anyone since Eve. She continued to use the excuse of harboring a broken heart.

"Maybe someday I'll know what that feels like."

"Really? That's nice to hear, Maggie."

Holy shit. Did she just say that out loud? She'd never thought of having children. Never wanted to be responsible for anyone else when she could barely take care of herself some days. So why the change of heart, and what the hell was she doing telling her father about it? She laughed to make it seem like a joke, even though that wasn't how it felt. "Probably not, Dad, but who knows."

"Whatever makes you happy, that's what you do, and you do it for you. Not me, your mom, or anyone else. Okay?"

The warmth of his words spread through her, and her vision blurred. There might have been many times she'd had doubts about what she was doing and where she was heading, but his love wasn't one of them and she was grateful for having been born into such a caring family. "Thanks."

They talked a few more minutes and she learned that her mom was off having a girls' night out with her friends, playing cards and drinking wine. After saying good-bye, Maggie wondered if Rayne's family was similar to her own, or at the other end of the spectrum, or somewhere in between. They hadn't shared much in the way of personal information, which was fine by her. Though, in the back of her mind there was an unexplainable itch to do just that. To get to know her better and to become, well, friends. In all honesty, Maggie didn't make a lot of friends. If she did, they'd ask questions and want to know things about her life that she didn't want to talk about. That's why she stuck to casual. It was easier that way, but it wasn't easier at all. It was harder. It was lonely.

But asking Rayne to join her for dinner was so out of character it had surprised her. What had moved her to act on the idea when she saw her standing outside with her face turned to the waning sunlight? She'd never been compelled to do so unless it was part of a pre-planned date that would end with sex. Funny, Maggie had no thoughts of sex being the motivation for the invitation. That itself was different. Rayne was different because she was focused inward and wanted her growing confidence in her body to instill confidence that she could handle whatever life threw at her. While they ate and shared bits of personal information the most telling thing Rayne had revealed was joining the singles pool, and Maggie got the impression it had been one-sided and unpleasant. Unless Rayne was an extremely talented actor, she was glad Rayne had used the experience for self-care initiatives. The only issue remaining was what Maggie was looking for, if anything other than companionship, from Rayne.

❖

Maggie's legs trembled. The last four miles of her six-mile circuit had been brutal and her way of punishing herself for a stupid mistake, all in the name of sex. She knew agreeing to see Tammy was a bad idea. It didn't matter that Tammy agreed that whatever happened was only going to happen once. Her physical need had led to the poor decision and didn't help matters. Maggie had been lonely before, but she'd never let her body take over her mind. This time the lust, the need to feel a warm body move beneath her, was too strong to resist, and when Tammy approached her following her HIT class, she said yes to the invitation. The simple response had turned into a night that ended badly. Tammy had all but locked her inside the apartment saying they'd been good together and why stop a good thing from lasting longer than one night. The sex *had* been fun if a little freaky. What wasn't fun was when Maggie got up to leave and Tammy had started begging, then screaming that she wasn't some bimbo to be used for sex, then thrown away. The only way she could escape was to promise she'd call. It was a lie she didn't tell in most circumstances, but when backed in a corner, she would do whatever it took to get away. The guilt of what she'd done, what she'd promised, made her more than a little sorry she'd been so easily swayed.

"If you think I'm doing that, you're crazy." Rayne stood to the side watching her, hands on her hips.

She slowed the machine to a walk for her cool down and wiped the rivulets of sweat from her face. Her heart rate began to level, but she didn't want to have the conversation she should be having with Rayne. Crossing lines led to someone being upset, and she couldn't be sure who that would be if she were to hook up with Rayne, though she couldn't imagine casual being anything Rayne would be interested in. The smile she shared was meant to assure Rayne, when in truth it was more to appease her own doubts and misgivings.

"I don't expect you to." Maggie knew she should stop there. "It's more of a punishment." She pursed her lips, sure she'd already said too much.

"Why do you need to be punished?" Rayne's question sounded innocent enough that Maggie almost shared the truth. Almost.

"I've been slacking off."

Rayne scoffed. "I doubt that. It certainly doesn't look that way to me." Rayne inhaled sharply while her ears reddened, and a flush of pink suffused her cheeks.

Even though the idea that Rayne's words meant she was looking at Maggie's body sent a jolt of heat through her, she refused to play into it. "Thanks." She stepped off the machine. "What are you working on today?"

Relief showed in Rayne's eyes at the change of topic. "It's elliptical day. Then maybe your class, but that depends on what your plans for me are because I don't want to feel like I'm going to die."

"I'd never push you that hard." She raised a brow. "But close." She chuckled. "Actually, I was going to mention the class. It's a great workout and I'm confident you can do it." The tabata routine was a mix of high-intensity interval training of eight sets of fast-paced exercises each performed for twenty seconds interspersed with a brief rest of ten seconds. This particular one was for beginners, but she wouldn't tell Rayne because she didn't want to make her feel self-conscious.

Rayne caught her lower lip between her teeth. "You really think so?"

She nodded. "I do." The look of uncertainty on Rayne's face eased and a small smile formed before she took a deep breath.

"Okay. Count me in."

Maggie's pulse quickened. "That's great. I'll see you in forty-five minutes at the mats." She needed a shower before she drove away her class members. "Rayne?"

"Yes?"

"Don't do more than twenty minutes on the elliptical and be sure to stretch before and after."

"Yes, ma'am."

The salute was instantaneous, and Maggie laughed out loud. "Carry on." As she headed with lighter steps toward the showers, the notion that she and Rayne could have something real sank in, making her sad all over again, and making her vow nothing good ever came from getting involved with members. So why did she continue to think Rayne might be the one exception?

CHAPTER EIGHT

She could do this. *She just had to.* Rayne's eyes burned as sweat dripped from her hairline and down her forehead. The first ten minutes had been hard, but not impossible. The next ten made her swear she'd never trust Maggie's assessment of her abilities again. The current set of exercises, the last before the cool down and stretch period, were absolutely going to kill her. The headline would read, "Woman keels over at tabata in attempt to prove to her trainer she could do it." No. Maggie wouldn't let her get to that point. She was smart and paid attention. There were only five people in the class, so it wasn't as if she could hide among the many.

"Good job, everyone. Last set. You've got this."

The torture continued for another five minutes. Rayne groaned. She didn't care if anyone heard her or not. When Maggie started clapping, she leaned over, hands on her trembling thighs, panting like she'd run a sprint race. The only thing that kept her upright was the embarrassment that would follow if she collapsed.

"Get some water and walk it out. If you cramp up, let me know." Maggie glowed. Her breathing wasn't labored nor was she profusely sweating like the rest of the class.

Rayne swore under her breath. They hadn't been in a one-on-one session. Maggie hadn't been singularly focused on her or pushing Rayne and telling her she was doing great. No problem. She didn't want the attention. She liked being one of the crowd, like always. But this felt different. It felt like she was back to being ordinary, and the courage she'd found to come to the gym in the first place seemed ages ago instead of a few weeks. Focusing on the fact that Maggie had approached her and offered to coach Rayne should have eased her mind. It still counted for something. It didn't matter that she was paying to have Maggie to herself for ten hours a week. She would have paid twice the amount Maggie quoted if it meant being next to a woman who was not only hot to look at but was warm and funny and charming. She was in a win-win situation, and she needed to remember Maggie had promised to get her where she wanted to be physically.

The night they'd gone to dinner had given her false hope that Maggie was interested in more than being her trainer. All through the meal, she'd been on pins and needles waiting for an invitation to go back to her place or follow Rayne home. The conversation had been pleasant and friendly, but lacked the wanton looks or innuendos that might indicate Maggie was interested in more than food. Rayne felt deflated after they parted ways, even with imagining Maggie had hesitated just long enough to give her the impression she was thinking about kissing her good-bye. A hand on her shoulder, a few words about how well she'd done in class, and a reminder to hydrate was all she got before they parted ways in the gym parking lot.

If her body wasn't showing signs of improvement, she would have blamed Maggie's lack of interest on that, but even she could tell her clothes fit better and the scale was inching downward. So, why *had* Maggie asked her to dinner? Did she feel sorry for her, or was Maggie the one who was lonely? That couldn't be it. All the women at the gym, even the straight ones, hung close to her, whispering to each other whenever Maggie was within sight.

Rayne couldn't blame them. Maggie would send anyone's heartrate into the danger zone, herself included. In her current state, Rayne was more concerned about her mental acuity. She was going a little crazy being around Maggie so much, and had no idea how to stop it.

❖

Rayne dropped onto the couch, head back, eyes closed. She couldn't put a finger on another time when she felt bone-tired like she did now. She'd survived Maggie's class and all the agony that went with it. Then there was that burst of adrenaline, making her wide-awake and full of energy—for about fifteen minutes. The exhilaration was followed by a hard crash, and by the time she finished showering, Rayne was dreading the ten-minute drive home. The whole time she questioned if she could do what seemed like the impossible. How was she going to survive five days a week of this for more than a month or two? Granted, she'd only had Maggie as her coach for a few weeks, but her stamina was bound to improve, and she wasn't going to take a class every day. Maggie had suggested one or two a week. More later down the road if she wanted muscle definition. *Definition.* She let out a half-hearted laugh. Survival. That was all she could think about at the moment.

Her stomach rumbled. It had been hours since lunch which consisted of an orange, half a tuna sandwich and some carrot sticks. Maggie had cautioned her on not sacrificing calories during the intense training phase, but Heather's words haunted her, and every morsel of food she put in her mouth was a reminder of the reason she was single. Being complacent at work was unacceptable and a worry she never suffered from. Her self-care had fallen down on the list of priorities, and now she was hell-bent on paying attention.

She glanced toward the kitchen. Whatever she had in the fridge and pantry wasn't going to satisfy her hunger. There were a lot of restaurant choices in the area, and she could easily walk to one, but the idea of expending any more energy was exhausting by itself. All she wanted to do was put on loungewear, curl up in the corner of the couch, and binge one of her favorite shows. That wasn't too much to ask. She'd been exercising regularly for the last few weeks and there wasn't a good reason not to indulge a bit. She could order so that there wouldn't be a ton of leftovers she'd feel forced to eat rather than throw it away.

"Fuck it."

Rayne got to her feet. Her leg muscles protested having to do any movement, but she made it to the pile of take-out menus and picked two of her favorite dishes of barbeque spare ribs and Budda's delight, a mixed vegetable dish in a brown sauce that she'd come to love. Next were her clothes. Rayne folded her barely worn outfit into her gym bag to use Monday, and chose the most comfortable, loose leggings and a worn T-shirt, sighing out loud as she slid the cotton over her body. The cursory glance into her cheval mirror reflected a woman who had embraced her right to be comfortable in her own skin. Heather could go to hell for all she cared when it came to her current attire.

She padded back to the fridge and stared at the open bottle of Riesling, chewing on her bottom lip. Adding calories to an already indulgent meal wasn't acting responsibly. Rayne shrugged before grabbing the bottle by the neck like she was trying to strangle the life out of it.

"If I'm going to splurge, I'm going all the way," Rayne said before pouring a modest amount into her favorite glass. She brought it to her nose and inhaled. Notes of citrus filled her nostrils, and her eyes closed as she let the aroma soothe her before taking a sip. "Oh yeah. I'm going to enjoy this meal."

The pile of items on the counter grew. Plate, paper towels, a fork, spoons, and a bowl for the bones. She carried it all with her wine to the coffee table, then turned on the TV. Rayne randomly flicked through the channels while she waited for the delivery. Her finger froze over the button when the screen filled with an advertisement for her gym, her eyes glued to the scenes that flashed in front of her, and she searched for Maggie in each one. Oh, there. Maybe. The camera moved to a different scene, and she'd only had a second or two to focus on the person in the background, but she could swear it was her, convinced she'd recognize her shape anywhere, anytime. The commercial ended and she blinked at the cat food ad that was running. How long had there been a commercial of Fitness by Finesse? Were there more? She so rarely watched TV it could have been up for months, and she'd never know.

❖

Maggie held the door open to give Rayne the opportunity to take the lead. The simple gesture would reveal how comfortable Rayne was in the role.

Rayne glanced up and smiled. "Thanks," she said before she walked through.

Nice.

"Fall will be here before we know it." Rayne pulled her scarf closer around her neck.

"For a northern born, you get cold easily." Maggie watched as Rayne narrowed her eyes as her lips thinned. She did the same thing when she was instructed to keep going. But no matter how much Maggie pushed her, Rayne didn't stop. Her dedication was awe-inspiring. Was there a ghost from her past chasing her? Something or someone she was trying to get away from or was it simply her wanting her physical strength to bolster her mental confidence. If there was a weakness within Rayne, she would bet money, that's where her biggest struggle lay.

"You just want a hot latte."

Rayne moaned. She whipped around to face her. "You know me too well," she said.

Oddly, the familiarity between them grew every day they were together. While they were a ways from being best friends, the feeling of letting someone close versus keeping people at a distance felt good.

Rayne batted her eyelashes mischievously. "So, will you join me?"

Maggie was about to say no, but Rayne looked so cute and shy and innocent, she couldn't. Besides, she wasn't the calorie police. If Rayne wanted a treat, she should have one. "I think that sounds wonderful."

Rayne grinned and clapped her hands, then skipped ahead. Just before she caught up to her, Rayne turned and said straight-faced, "Sucker."

"Hey," Maggie called out as Rayne took off again. Peals of laughter drifted back to her on the air currents. There were glimpses of this side of Rayne that made her want Rayne as her friend. Someone she could depend on when she felt like she had too much to carry alone, because alone was getting to be a drag.

❖

"That was divine," Rayne said then drained her paper cup and tossed it in the nearby recycle bin.

"Glad you enjoyed it." Maggie had opted for an iced chai latte. She had the chills just thinking about it.

"How long have you worked at the gym?"

Maggie took a minute. "Five years, give or take."

"It's obvious you enjoy it." She wasn't used to prying in other people's business. Scientists were a quirky bunch and weren't into talking about themselves much. She'd spent the last week doing overnight experiments, and the endless documentation had left her fatigued and needing a conversation that didn't revolve around statistics and hypotheses.

"I guess." Maggie shrugged. "I kind of fell into the position and it stuck."

Goals were good and Rayne believed everyone should have a few. "Is there something you'd rather do?"

Maggie was quiet for a long beat before pointing to a bench in front of a closed bakery shop. She leaned forward with her elbows on her thighs and took a deep breath. "I'd like to open my own wellness center. One that offers massages, acupuncture, tai chi. Things that support the mind and body in concert."

"That's a great idea." Rayne heard melancholy in Maggie's tone. "So, when are you going to open?"

"Who knows." Maggie sighed. "I need an investor before I can start. I have a business plan, but no one I've asked is interested in dropping the necessary cash to get it off the ground."

"You don't know anyone?"

Maggie shook her head. "The women who want to…" She trailed off. "No. No one."

The idea that women had offered money and Maggie had refused their help led her to believe that maybe the rumors about Maggie being a player were exaggerated, giving her a sense of relief, though she wasn't sure why.

Rayne knew all about needing funding. Research needed a constant influx of money to keep experiments going and the staff to carry them out. Rayne was lucky to be in a lab that had both and she was hoping to get a grant for "rising scientists" from the National Institutes of Health to get to the next level and duplicate her initial results. She knew the science part of it, but writing it down step-by-step and sharing her hypotheses with the people who had the power to turn her down was the part she was unsure of.

"Have you tried to get a grant?"

"I wouldn't have any idea how to even start."

It was Rayne's turn to think. "I know some people who have applied for all types of money from a lot of different sources. I'd be happy to check into it." That was what friends did, right?

"That's generous of you, but I don't know. It sounds like a lot of work."

"It is, unless you know people."

"You mean like guys who put the screws to the people who cross them."

Rayne laughed heartily. "You watch too much TV."

"I do not," Maggie said indignantly.

"Whatever. Anyway, you already have a business plan. That's a great start." She placed her hand on Maggie's arm. "Please?"

"You do know your charm isn't going to get you everything you want."

She patted Maggie's arm and stood. "That doesn't mean I'm going to stop."

Maggie laughed and shook her head. "Shall we continue our walk?"

"Only if you say yes to my helping."

"Why does it feel like a bribe."

Rayne fought against smiling. "You said it, not me." Truth was, she wanted to do something special for Maggie. With her confidence growing in her abilities to endure, came the desire to see others reach achievements they might have once thought impossible. She would have never guessed it, but Maggie had revealed self-doubt tonight and that took a level of trust. The kind of trust people shared when building friendships. Rayne had no intention of letting Maggie down.

CHAPTER NINE

I can't."

"You can. I've seen how strong you are. Push." Maggie's style of training was tough, encouraging each person to do more than they thought possible. She watched and learned what was true inability versus fear of failure. Rayne was on the brink of fear getting the best of her and Maggie's job was to get her past the fear and through that barrier to accomplishment. Rayne dropped out of her plank and rolled to her back, just shy of the ninety second mark, her breathing labored. This was not the same Rayne who had tackled a steep incline hike just a few days ago.

"Sorry," Rayne said. The look of disappointment saddened her.

"You don't have to apologize." Maggie helped her sit up and grabbed Rayne's water bottle for her. She took a few gulps, but made no move to get up, another indication that Rayne was out of sorts. She bent down. "What's going on?"

Rayne wiped sweat from her face, then shook her head. "Nothing."

She glanced around to see if anyone was close. "I know better. This isn't nothing." Maggie pointed to where Rayne was on the mat, still looking like the world had stopped turning.

"My paper was rejected."

The look of defeat was in full bloom and Rayne looked on the brink of tears. "Please tell me what that means." She helped Rayne stand.

Rayne took another drink, then slammed down the bottle. "It means the backing for digging into my hypothesis isn't there, so there's no point in submitting a grant application."

Maggie understood enough of the way a grant worked from conversations they'd had. Without proof Rayne was on the right track she would likely not receive financial backing. Much like her own situation, investors were skeptical there would be enough interest in the wellness center to keep the ledger in the black.

"Can't you send the paper elsewhere? Or make changes so they accept it?"

Rayne drank the last of her water, hand on her hip. "That would be the usual thing to do." She turned and headed to the locker room.

Maggie followed, desperate to give Rayne her support. "Rayne, wait."

When Rayne looked up, her eyes were filled with unshed tears.

"Hey," she said as she lightly gripped Rayne's shoulders. "What's really going on?" When Rayne didn't response, she guided her to a bench. "Whatever it is, it will feel less of a burden if you share it."

Rayne swiped at her eyes. "Everything I did this week went to shit."

Touching Rayne's face would have been too familiar a gesture. Maggie took her hand instead. "That happens sometimes."

"Does it ever happen to you?" Rayne sniffled.

"More than I care to admit."

Rayne smiled tentatively. "That's hard to believe."

"Honestly, it's time you believe you can do anything, and I'm not just talking about the gym. Worrying doesn't resolve things out of your control, Rayne."

"It feels like a failure."

Maggie had to find another way to get through to her. "Why? Because your original idea didn't pan out? Or could it have been because whoever looked at it didn't understand what you were trying to do?"

Rayne took a deep breath. "Or a dozen other reasons."

"Okay. You can try again, right? Submit it somewhere else or do more of whatever it is you do to prove some scientific theory."

She waved her hand. Rayne had tried to explain terms and ideas in a way that she could relate to, but it was still a foreign language to her.

"You don't really comprehend how science works, do you?' Rayne smiled.

"Not if my life depended on it." She laughed and Rayne joined her.

"That's okay. There are moments when I don't either." Rayne stood. "Thanks for the pep talk." She opened her locker and grabbed her toiletry bag. "I'm going to take a nice hot shower before trying to do anymore deep thinking."

Maggie was tempted to take her out for a drink to help her unwind before thinking twice about it. The only time she did that with a client was when she had plans to sleep with them. Rayne was becoming more than a client, and Maggie could use a friend in her life. She turned away.

"Maggie?"

She stopped and glanced over her shoulder. "Hmm?"

"Thank you for being a friend."

Here heart beat a little faster and she wondered if Rayne could read her thoughts. "You're welcome. Try not to beat yourself up. You'll find a way."

Rayne nodded. "Some days are easier than others, but I'll try."

❖

Rayne ripped the page out of the notebook and added it to the growing stack. She left the gym in a hurry, barely waving good-bye to Maggie before running to her car. The shower was soothing, giving her a chance to clear her mind and look at work issues from a different angle. She'd just dried her hair when a new method of proving her hypothesis had struck, and there was no time to lose for getting it down on paper.

Good thing she always had a ready supply in her backpack. She jotted the basic synopsis down and hurried home so she could expand on how she could isolate a new pathway to the T-cells that regulated the body's response to an invasion by pathogens. Rayne had always been fascinated by how the human body worked and questioned what made the well-oiled machine misfire on occasion. While no one could give her a definitive answer, she did learn that cell responses could be manipulated in certain situations, and the way to find how, where, when, and why lay within the framework of science.

One more page and her mind needed a break, her body crying out for food. She rambled to the refrigerator and hoped there would be a palatable leftover. Her energy level was plummeting from the physical and mental exertion she'd spent. She'd given up during her workout, which until today had not happened since Maggie had become her trainer. Her face heated. She'd never doubted Maggie knew what she was capable of and how far to push her. She deserved Rayne's best effort every day.

Instead of becoming upset or angry at her lack-luster performance, Maggie had been encouraging, kind, and understanding. Rayne chuckled. She'd even tried to throw around a few of the terms Rayne had explained to help her understand what she did at work. For as smart as Maggie was about so many things, it appeared the reasoning behind science eluded her. Rayne was endeared by how much she tried, nonetheless.

The contents of the take-out container were not only recognizable, but she also knew it was only a few days old and prime for the taking. She dumped the chicken and broccoli on top of the white rice and shoved it into the microwave. Three minutes seemed too long to wait. Rayne stood with the refrigerator door open and looked at her choices. Water. Juice. Skim milk. White wine.

"Ugh. Why do you have to tempt me?"

She chewed her lower lip. One small glass would get her through dinner.

"What the hell."

As the microwave dish spun and the power level rose and fell, Rayne restrained from emptying the bottle and settled on a short pour. She hadn't finished her workout. She was going to have to do better if she wanted more. She placed the steaming bowl on a potholder and brought it and the wine to the living room.

"A little mindless surfing would be a great way to end a useless day."

Not useless. She'd thanked Maggie for being a friend. "Damn." She let her head fall onto the back of the couch. Great. The first woman she'd found crush-worthy and she'd all but told her the "we can be friends" line, meaning "I think we'd make great friends but not fuck buddies." She was going to have to revamp her toy collection if this was going to be her MO with hot women. Not like it mattered. She didn't have the courage to pursue a relationship after the last disaster. It's not like Maggie had made anything close to resembling a flirty remark or a strategically placed touch. They were destined to be friends. She could live with that.

"Were you serious about helping with grant funding?" Maggie asked. She had applied for a business loan at a local bank, hoping her willingness to invest in their shared community would give her an edge. Yet, she was a realist. The financial climate wasn't conducive to promoting a somewhat unknown capital venture. If she were in California she'd have a better shot, but she had no interest in moving.

Rayne had just finished her routine and was doing a cooldown lap around the parking lot. "Of course." Rayne stopped in front of her. "I think your best bet is trying for either a woman-owned business grant or an entrepreneur grant for your wellness clinic." Rayne tipped her head to one side, her eyes gazing upward. "NASA gives a lot of funds to projects that have nothing to do with space, but centers around the overall health of their astronauts, medical and otherwise. If you target your goal around how treating mind, body, and spirit factor into better performance I don't see how they can turn you down."

The concept sounded masterful. She didn't want Rayne doing the actual writing. What she needed most was guidance in the wording and how to appeal to the funding source. "Are there any resources or guidelines in how to put all my ideas to paper?"

Rayne leaned against her car. "I have an NIH Grant Writing handbook you can borrow. It's fairly reader friendly and will give you an outline to follow if that's what you're looking for."

"Yes, it is. I have a bunch of pieces and parts of what I want to do and how it would look in the physical world, but they're unorganized and rough." This was Rayne's wheelhouse. "If I can use the handbook to get the bulk of it down, would you mind reading it through and help smoothing it out to a document that will appeal to the people who make those decisions?"

Rayne smiled. "I'll be happy to help in whatever way you want. Reviewers are sometimes a mix of people who have no scientific background, but who are critical thinkers in how a concept might be worth investing in." Rayne tapped her index finger against her lower lip. Maggie could almost see the wheels turning. "You'll have to write a progress report, but once you've done one, that part is easy enough." Suddenly, Rayne pushed off and grasped her arm, her face animated and her eyes sparkling. "You should ask for multi-year funding. A business needs more than a year to get off the ground and build a clientele."

"You're making my head spin."

"That's how I feel every time I think about writing a paper. It's just part of the process."

"If you say so."

"I do. I'll get the book to you. Take your time pulling it together and when you have a draft, we'll sit down and look it over."

"Thank you."

They headed back inside. The entire process sounded daunting, but she wasn't having any luck doing what she'd been doing to find a business partner. What did she have to lose?

CHAPTER TEN

I was thinking about going to the downtown spring festival Sunday. Care to join me?" Maggie asked.

Rayne swirled the contents in her paper cup. "I don't know, Mags. I should be in the lab." She didn't seem all that enthused about her current project.

"Everyone needs a break, including you. A few hours away won't hurt, will it?" She knew Rayne was still disheartened by a lack of the anticipated results she'd been hoping for with an experiment. No matter how many times she told her it didn't mean she was failing, Rayne continued to feel less than capable in her career choice.

"There's something I'm missing. Steve and I have both gone over the sequence. On paper it looks sound, but when it comes to testing the theory, the results are all over the place." Rayne shook her head. "I don't know what to do."

She took Rayne's hands and stood. "I know what we're going to do." Maggie wrapped her arm around Rayne's shoulder, gently pulling her into a side hug. Rayne bumped into her and sighed.

"Let's hear it." Rayne hip checked her, then slid from under her arm.

"Let's go to the Station. There's decent food and, best of all, it's line dancing night." Maggie loved to dance, and it had been ages since she'd had a dedicated group of dance partners who were great at teaching, too.

"Line dancing?" Rayne looked at her incredulously. "Did I forget to mention I also have two left feet."

She looked down and studied Rayne's feet. "They look fine to me."

Rayne's frustration showed on her face, her lips pursed into a thin line.

"Look, you can't keep up this pace and not suffer, emotionally and physically. You've been doing extra workouts, which means you're sacrificing another part of your day. If I were a bettor, I'd say it's one of two things. You're either sacrificing sleep or down time. Maybe both. That's not sustainable, Rayne." In the face of possibly making a mistake by sending the wrong signal, Maggie lifted Rayne's chin until their eyes met. "A little self-care may be just what you need." The color of Rayne's eyes deepened, and she watched the internal struggle play out. Finally, Rayne's shoulders relaxed, and a smile formed.

"You know being right most of the time is damn annoying."

She slid her hand away. "It's one of my many charms."

"Modesty is not." Rayne laughed without restraint.

"Does that mean you're coming along?"

Rayne nodded. "How could I possibly resist."

Maggie wanted to jump up and down. It had been a longshot when she brought up the idea, but now that Rayne was going, she was more excited than she thought she would be. "Yes." She resisted fist-pumping. "Let's go."

"Whoa, cowgirl. I'm not going like this." Rayne put her hands on her hips.

How long would it take her to get ready? She glanced at her phone. The dancing started in twenty minutes. "You look great." Maggie snatched Rayne's hand and pulled her along. "Come on. They're going to be starting soon."

"I'm sure they'll let us join in whenever we get there."

"Rayne, please. The start is, well, magical." She stumbled on the line dancing group by accident and had been meaning to go back to see if she still enjoyed it. In her eyes, there was nothing to compare to the dance that started the night, whatever it might be.

Rayne stared at her with a quizzical expression, her head tipped to one side."

"What are we waiting for." Rayne gave her a light shove. "Let's go."

Maybe she shouldn't be wishing there might someday be more than a shared friendship between them, but for now what they had was pretty damn cool. "You can ride shotgun," she said as she held the car door open, then ran to the other side. She felt like a kid without a care in the world.

❖

If there was one thing Rayne would have never imagined as fun, it would be this. Granted, it hadn't started great because she really did have two left feet when it came to dancing, but with Maggie at her side and a patient group of dancers, she managed to find a number of steps to follow.

The best part though, was seeing the pure joy on Maggie's face. She was a natural-born dancer for the choreographed steps. Her long, fluid lines and lower body strength moved to the rhythm that had taken Rayne most of the night to find. Line dancing was not for the faint of heart. Sweat trickled down her back as she drank water while watching Maggie and the others perform an intricate pattern of steps. They made it look easy. Sitting this one out had been the correct decision.

"No matter how many times I've tried I can't get the last sequence right." A woman with blond hair piled on the top of her head stood next to her with her hands on her hips, panting.

"I'm not sure if I'd get any of it." The hoping and slapping of their heels were a blur of frenzied movements.

"Give it time." The woman stuck out her hand. "Hi, I'm Sally." Rayne took the offer. "Nice to meet you, Sally. I'm Rayne."

"Pleasure." Sally watched as the steps sped up to an even faster crescendo before the final beat. "Woot, woot. Way to go." Sally clapped and hooted as the floor cleared and walked towards the man she'd been sitting with earlier. Maggie came to where she stood, all smiles.

"That was fun!" Maggie poured a cup of water from the pitcher on the table and drank it down. Her breathing was fast, and a light mist of sweat covered her face.

"You look good out there."

"Thanks. It's been ages. I haven't line danced since…" Maggie's expression went from animated to sober, a shadow darkening her eyes. "Not for years." She turned away.

Rayne wanted to ask if she was okay, but the veil that had dropped kept her from asking. Whatever Maggie was going to say had died on her lips and that usually meant what she was remembering was unpleasant. If Maggie wanted to share what it was with her, she would do it when she was ready. Rayne respected her need to keep the memory close. She had a few herself.

"They're just about to wrap it up. I'm going to get a beer. Would you like something?" Maggie took a paper towel from the stack and wiped her face, neck, and arms.

"Whatever you're having."

Though Maggie smiled, it appeared melancholy. "Be right back." Instead of going to the bar, Maggie turned down the short hall to the restrooms and disappeared.

Maybe I should go after her. Rayne was torn. On the one hand, the intrusion might not be welcome. On the other, isn't that what a friend would do?

"My turn to buy a round," Sally said as she juggled a half-dozen empty bottles.

"Let me help you." Rayne snagged a couple of precariously tucked bottles.

"Thanks. Can I get you a drink?"

She shook her head. "Maggie's getting me one." She set the bottles on the bar just as Maggie approached.

"I see you've made a friend." Maggie's smile was genuine.

"This is Sally." Sally was just finishing giving her order to the bartender.

"Hi, Sally. I'm Maggie."

"Can I buy you both a drink?"

"Maybe another time," Maggie said as she pulled a twenty from her pocket.

Rayne placed her hand on Maggie's forearm. The muscle beneath twitched. "If you're ready to go, so am I."

Maggie glanced at their connection. "You don't mind?"

She chuckled, more to lighten the mood than because it was funny. "I'm sweaty and hungry. A shower and a snack sound really good right now."

After a minute of hesitation, Maggie tucked away the money. "That sounds good."

Rayne gathered her things and waved good-bye to the other dancers. Maggie promised to return soon, and she wondered if Maggie would go on a regular basis, since she was good at it and had a lot of fun. She, on the other hand, wouldn't mind an occasional night but didn't see it as a regular part of her routine. She had enough going on, and one more commitment might be overwhelming. Unless Maggie kept asking her to join in like friends sometimes did.

❖

The last few weeks dragged by. Nothing went right and the pile of work on Rayne's desk kept growing. When the clock on the computer screen displayed 5:01 p.m., she couldn't get out the door fast enough. The elevator tested her patience while she pulled on her light coat and smiled. Friday night meant meeting up with Maggie for a movie and a late dinner. It had started almost two months ago as a way to celebrate Rayne's successes at the gym and they always had such a good time together. The line dancing that Maggie enjoyed wasn't her thing, but that was okay. Their friendship had blossomed at a fast pace, and now they would often text with funny anecdotes or inquiries as to how the day was going. It was nice having a friend to hang out and relax with.

On a different note, rumor had it Heather's attempt to "make it to the top by starting on her knees," got her in a bit of hot water and she'd been transferred out of the main office to some obscure town on the West Coast. One more reason to smile. Karma was sometimes a bitch who bit you in the ass, and Rayne congratulated the cosmos on homing in on another deserving victim.

As she strode toward her car parked on the upper level, Rayne liked how her thighs flexed and warmed on the incline since she'd been going to the gym, and her thoughts wandered to the early morning dream from when she was first starting to develop a relationship with Maggie. A burst of internal sparks traveled along her nerves. *Maggie*. Aside from Rayne not having climaxed at the time, not seeing her nude was frustrating. She enjoyed Maggie's sense of humor. Her innate ability to know when Rayne had doubts, and gave her the encouragement she needed to push through like the time they went for a hike and Rayne almost gave up.

"We're almost there and I'm not leaving you behind." Maggie descended to where Rayne was bent over, sucking wind.

"Go ahead. I can't make it up there." She tried to straighten, but the pain in her side stole her breath again.

Maggie pulled her bottle from her pack, shook a packet of electrolytes in it and shook vigorously. "Drink this slowly and take deep breaths."

She didn't want to be stuck on the side of a mountain, and she definitely didn't want to be left behind even if she did say it. "Okay," she gasped, then concentrated on her breathing. When she recovered a bit, she drank intermittently, keeping her hand on her affected side and gingerly stood upright.

"You're doing great." Maggie pointed up the steep incline. "The view will take your breath in a whole different way."

Granted, it was only a few hundred feet, but the last few had tested not only her strength, it had also made her doubt she'd ever be able to do it again without feeling like she was dying. "If it's not, you owe me." She finished the drink.

"You got it." Maggie finished her own bottle. "Shake out your muscles and remember, it's not a race. Keep a steady pace by watching your footing and where you're going, not the destination."

She'd made it to the top and was awed by the vista in front of her. Maggie had been right. The view had been worth the struggle to get there. The mountain canyon divided the thick forest and the field of wildflowers that sloped to the valley floor.

Maggie was kind and thoughtful. And damn, she was hot as hell. The idea that she was everything Rayne had ever dared to imagine as a partner was terrifying. Mostly because the thought of messing up another relationship filled her with fear. The horror stories she'd heard about good friends who turned into people who despised each other after becoming lovers were rampant, but so were the friends to lovers population, and she'd always believed it was the best way to start a relationship. Did she dare wish that for herself? As she drove the short distance to the theater, Rayne gave herself the same lecture that had become her go-to whenever she thought of Maggie in more than what they shared now. Maggie *might* be the perfect partner, but she was an amazing friend. Rayne was okay with the way things were.

Fingers lightly caressed Rayne's inner thigh, traveling upward before resting on her hip. Another breath and the hand lifted her leg followed by warm, soft lips kissing her calf, behind her knee, drawing out small gasps. A low moan sounded deep in her throat before a finger sank slowly into her slick opening, making her hips reflexively rise from the bed as her hands grabbed at the sheets. She was just about to say Heather's name when her eyes opened.

Maggie looked at her with the kind of wanton desire that had never been present in Heather's eyes. Accompanying the gaze was a palpable need that couldn't be mistaken for anything else. The pure pleasure of the moment reflected in Maggie's eyes, like liquid gold. Confusion coursed through her. How had they ended up in bed together? Rayne grappled for the sequence of events, but everything was blurry, out of focus.

"Mags…?" she whispered into the darkness.

Maggie was on her knees between Rayne's legs. She slid her finger out and licked it. "I've been wanting to do this for a long time." Her eyes never left Rayne's as she repeated the action with two fingers, delightfully filling her, and she ground her ass against the warm sheet beneath her.

Rayne's vision blurred as Maggie stroked deeper. She was getting close to climaxing. The alarm began its loud, annoying beep and her heart nearly stopped. "Shit! Shit! Shit!" She silenced the intrusive bastard, but what she really wanted was to throw it out the door. "First erotic dream I've ever had, and I didn't even get to come! Damn it!" Rayne threw back the covers and was about to get up when she remembered who had been kneeling between her spread thighs in the dream.

"No, no, no!" She rolled over and buried her head in the pillows. Desperate to erase the vision, she willed it to be someone else. Anyone except Maggie. Rayne flipped onto her back and stared at the ceiling. Maggie had never given any indication she was attracted to her. *It's just an overactive imagination.* That, and not having sex in what was forever. Okay. So maybe forever was a chronological exaggeration, but it felt that long. *Wait until I tell Mags about this one.* She was going to die laughing. Wait. What? She couldn't tell Maggie.

"Uh-uh. We aren't going there. Nope. Not doing it."

Not having convinced anyone, Rayne got moving. She had an all-day experiment that would force her to concentrate on something other than her hot trainer fucking her.

"That was…enlightening," Maggie said about the movie as she strode easily beside Rayne. Her hand occasionally brushed Rayne's knuckle, reminding her of *the* dream. "Hey, you okay?" Maggie turned to face her just before reaching the entrance to the little bistro they'd agreed on for dinner. Her face registered concern.

Admittedly, Rayne had been pretty preoccupied by thoughts of a naked Maggie on and off for a while. The last thing she wanted to do was reveal the spike in her libido and make her uncomfortable. Or worse, lose her friendship. "Yeah. Just tired, I guess. It was a rough week."

Maggie took her hand and gave it a gentle shake. "I know exactly what you need!" she said a little too excitedly.

Rayne's cheeks heated at her own thoughts about *exactly what she needed*. Careful not to make it obvious, she pulled her hand away. "Umm, what would that be, Mags?" She tried to make her voice light and frivolous. She doubted she pulled it off, but Maggie had the good graces to ignore the way it came out.

"A bottle of our favorite wine."

She smiled with genuine affection, though disappointment registered on the inside. "I think you might be right, Mags." It certainly couldn't hurt numb the internal turmoil she was in. She hated keeping secrets, and this was a big one.

CHAPTER ELEVEN

The restaurant was packed. For once, Rayne was at a loss for the small talk that normally came so easily. While they waited, she opted for scrolling through her phone, pretending there was riveting information she just *had* to read. She didn't want to think about having sex with Maggie when there was no outward sign Maggie wanted anything more than friendship. After twenty minutes of near silence sprinkled with an occasional grunt here and there, they were led to a small booth in the back corner that they liked to think of as theirs. Maggie ordered a bottle of vintage wine along with several appetizers. The fact that Maggie's actions were what usually happened when they went out to eat more often than not, made her think about what constituted a couple, which then led to vividly reliving her dream.

Rayne was grateful for the seclusion. Her skin crawled at the thought that everyone was staring at her, making her uncomfortable holding the secret, and keeping silent made it all the more unbearable. What would happen if Maggie knew about her X-rated dream? Would she be as mortified at the discovery as Rayne was for having it? Well, not mortified of course. She enjoyed the visions because Maggie was hot as hell and the kind of woman she was attracted to. Funny, smart, thoughtful, and confident. She'd instilled that same kind of confidence in Rayne at every opportunity, telling her she was more capable than she believed. But still, true or not, Maggie was her friend first and she needed to remember that.

"To friendship and whatever comes our way." Maggie held up her glass in toast.

The memory of how flustered she'd been when she saw her at the gym, then spoke with her in person, might have made her run if it had been a few months ago, but she hadn't been able to. Maggie's enigmatic personality drew her in. Rayne had gotten over that initial shyness, but even now when she should have glanced away, nothing could stop her from searching Maggie's eyes for a sign she was having similar thoughts.

Rayne didn't trust her voice. Instead she picked up her goblet in salute, lightly tapping Maggie's before she took a long swallow. It was crisp and clean. The pear and apple flavors were enjoyable and light on her tongue. It was perfect. Like Maggie. *Stop it!* Rayne must have made a face because Maggie set her glass down before leaning in, her voice a low, deep rumble that made keeping quiet all the harder. "Is the wine okay?"

"It's really good." She chewed her bottom lip.

"Please tell me what has you out of sorts tonight."

She had nowhere to hide. Maggie wanted answers and she wouldn't lie to her. Her friendship was too important to disregard the question. Rayne sucked at hiding her true feelings, and her only alternative was to try to brush off the enormity of what she was so close to telling her.

"It's nothing really. Just a dream, that's all." Rayne looked over the rim of her glass and took a sip. Maggie did not seem convinced. The waiter provided a reprieve by delivering the appetizers. As a diversionary tactic, she pointed to the dishes. "I'm starving!" Her proclamation was a little too loud and she knew it was forced, but she continued to ignore the question in Maggie's gaze. She reached for a stuffed clam and Maggie's hand closed over her outstretched one.

"Stop. Please tell me."

Rayne placed the clam on her plate and sat back. "Fine." She decided to tell a white lie. Not something she did often and she'd likely feel guilty afterward, but it's what she needed to do for both their sakes. "Promise not to laugh?"

One side of her beautiful mouth curled into a barely controlled smile. "I promise." Maggie crossed her heart as if to make her point.

Rayne nodded. "I had a dream…" Her mouth went dry. After a drink of water, she gathered her thoughts.

Maggie broke the brief silence, encouraging her to keep going. "Yes, I got that part. Go on."

Heat traveled up her neck. She swallowed hard. "You were in the dream with me." Rayne hoped that was enough to satisfy the inquiry. She knew better. Maggie was naturally curious and not easily put off.

"What were we doing?" Maggie smiled, as she reached for bruschetta.

It was an innocent enough question. Rayne wanted to puke. Maybe she could pretend to go to the restroom and leave. No. That would be downright rude and not something she was willing to do. There wasn't any easy way out of having the conversation, so she opted for vagueness and a plausible alternative.

"We were at the gym." She dove into the clam. If she kept eating she wouldn't have to go on. Right?

Maggie dropped her fork on the plate, startling her and garnering the attention of nearby diners. "Would you PLEASE tell the whole story? There's something bothering you tonight and I need to know what it is," she said. Frustration wasn't something Rayne had ever witnessed from Maggie, and the idea that she had caused it due to her hedging didn't sit well. Maggie deserved the truth, and not giving it was disrespectful and dishonest.

"Oh alright." Rayne huffed as though she'd been caught doing something nefarious. "You were telling me I could lift the weight, but I couldn't and…" She leaned in to whisper so only Maggie heard what she was about to say. "you saved me from serious injury. Then I tried another machine, but every time I failed and you had to rescue me in some way." By the time she finished, Rayne could feel the heat of her embarrassment from her neck to her ears.

"It was just a dream, Rayne." Maggie reached for her hand on the table, and she slid it away. The last thing she needed was Maggie's touch. The gesture registered on Maggie's face, but she kept going. "You are a beautiful, capable woman. After everything you've accomplished, there should be no doubts."

Maggie's certainty made her feel worse than the lie. The need to get herself together forced her to her feet. "Excuse me. I need to use the restroom." Rayne didn't wait for Maggie to say anything else. What could she say? The dream fantasy where Maggie was the star was burned on the inside of her eyelids, and every time she closed them, Maggie was there. If Maggie knew the truth, would she still be there?

CHAPTER TWELVE

The time alone gave Maggie an opportunity to think. Until hearing Rayne had been dreaming about failing, she'd been doing well by not giving in to her growing attraction. She definitely didn't want to fall into her habit of the occasional pickup at the local queer bar or engaging in an NSA (no strings attached) rendezvous with a client wasn't going to happen in this case. The scary part of knowing she didn't want to go there with Rayne made the situation even more complicated. Not engaging with her sexually was for the best because every time she'd had the flutter—like the ones she used to have with Eve—let her know she wasn't ready for a relationship. Maybe she never would be, and the longer she went unattached the more she accepted this could be her life for the duration.

It wasn't that bad. Things could be a lot worse. In fact, a lot of people would jump at the opportunity to have her life. She got to work with beautiful women, have sex when she wanted, and still maintained her independence. Win-win, except for the times when loneliness encroached on her near-perfect life and the other side of her bed was empty and cold. Those moments sucked.

The bigger question was what she was going to do about Rayne in the present because pondering about the future wasn't a thought she wanted to entertain, no matter how appealing it was. She took another sip of wine. Rayne emerged from the hallway and slowly walked toward their table. Maggie was convinced the best thing she could do was take control of the situation.

"Dreams are just that, Rayne. It's where our imagination can run wild." She didn't want to hurt Rayne's feelings, but she also couldn't take the chance of Rayne becoming more reliant on her than for training or the current friendship they shared. "I enjoy our time together, in and out of the gym. We have a great relationship, but I think you need more in your life." Rayne stared at her for a long time and Maggie could almost see her mind trying to decipher what she wasn't saying. It was all conjecture and projection on her part. She wished she was clairvoyant and knew what Rayne was thinking. Maybe it was better to not know.

"That's why I didn't want to tell you about it. I mean sure, it was silly, but it might make us both feel…awkward." Rayne's smile was tight and definitely forced. Maggie didn't want anything forced between them.

"Okay, I get that." It wasn't okay. None of the emotions that were making her stomach churn were okay.

"Okay?" Rayne asked. The look in her eyes was hopeful as she reached for her wine.

"Yes. I won't let a dream interfere with your training or our friendship," she said as she poured more wine into both glasses. "You need to find another way to prove your subconscious doubts are unfounded."

Even though Rayne's cheeks flushed, she giggled. "Not likely, but I'll keep that in mind."

"Okay then." Maggie raised her glass again. "To being done with being awkward for tonight." With the toast, there was obvious relief on Rayne's face and Maggie liked knowing she'd done the right thing by putting her to ease. "Let's pick out entrees while we finish our apps. I don't know about you, but I'm ravenous."

An hour later, Maggie was doing her best to be in the moment and failing miserably. It wasn't her imagination. The air around her was thick and uncomfortable. Unspoken words floated on the current with the weight of her denial heavy on her shoulders. She did want more with Rayne, and pursuing it would likely ruin everything. "I think you should get out there." Wow. That was anything but subtle.

"Excuse me?" Rayne set her fork down.

"You've made so much progress and you should be confident in your capabilities, so it's a good time to get back in the dating scene."

Rayne blinked several times. "Oh." She glanced down at her near empty plate. "I haven't really thought about it."

"It will be good for you."

"I don't have time to date." Rayne finally made eye contact. "Between work and the gym, not to mention taking care of house stuff, I'm already stretched thin."

She waved Rayne's excuses off. "You could make time. One night or day here and there. That would be good to start."

"I don't know. My wardrobe is as limited as my time."

"Then you need a shopping trip first. I'm sure you're dying to try on some new styles."

Rayne took a deep breath. "Shopping alone isn't any fun."

Maggie sat back as the waiter took their plates.

"Would you like coffee?" The waiter asked.

She nodded. "Rayne?"

"Yes, please."

"We'd like to look at the dessert menu, too." Maggie swallowed around the knot in her throat. The idea of Rayne getting back into the dating scene should have made her happy. The perfect representation of Rayne's confidence coming into play.

"Of course," the waiter said, the entire length of his arm lined with plates.

"What about your best friend? What's her name? Syd?"

"Cybil. She's out of the country and won't be back for months." Rayne looked defeated.

"If you don't mind me tagging along, I'll keep you company."

Rayne chewed her lip in that nervous, sexy way she did when she wanted to do something but wasn't sure of herself. "I don't know."

"I'm not saying I'm going to try on a dress, but I know when I see something I like. Come on, it'll be fun. Scout's honor." She made the hand sign.

The burst of laughter from Rayne broke the remaining tension, and Maggie joined in with her own laugh. When she settled, she pushed a little more. "Well?"

"You're impossible."

"I know. I'm hard to resist."

Rayne growled. Her belly tightened in response. "Fine, but not one more word about dating until I have something decent to wear."

She opened her mouth, intent on getting her point across, but Rayne wasn't having it.

"Not one word."

The waiter set steaming cups of coffee, sugar, and cream on the table before handing them small menus offering six desserts, each one more decadent than the one above.

"Want to share one?" she asked, knowing full well that the inuendo was blatant.

Rayne's lips pursed before the corners of her mouth lifted into a smile. "What did you have in mind?"

Maggie couldn't help wondering that if Rayne knew what she was thinking, this night would end much differently than by simply sharing a dessert. "You pick." Deferring to Rayne was the only choice because if it were up to her, she'd invite Rayne back to her place and that never ended well. But what if it did?

CHAPTER THIRTEEN

S o, what are you going to do about it?" Cybil asked over the shitty international internet connection.

The idea that she was going shopping with Maggie rather than her best friend had driven Rayne to try every possible way to talk with Cybil. She sat at an outside table of a little out-of-the-way café in Peru where it had taken her twenty-five minutes to find the one spot where there was a connection. Kinda.

"You aren't helping."

"Isn't that why you were desperate to talk with me? So I could help you figure out what you were going to do about this fatal attraction with McDreamie?"

"Stop. Her name is Maggie and there isn't any attraction in the mix. She *told* me to date, for God's sake."

Cybil sighed over the flickering camera image that was grainy. "You're so out of practice."

"With what?" She had an idea, but she needed to hear it to make it real.

"Recognizing when a woman is interested in you. If I ever see Heather again, I'm going to kill her for ruining a fully functional BF and turning her into a hesitant, unsure, wannabe lesbian."

The words were like a slap in the face. Not that she didn't need it. Talking with Cybil was the one thing that would jerk her out of the muddy waters where she was trying to see the bottom while knowing it was impossible. "I'm a lesbian!"

"Really? Then tell me what you're going to do."

There were an endless number of possibilities floating around in her head. "Go shopping with Maggie?"

"That's a start. What will you do when Maggie realizes she was wrong and doesn't want you dating anyone but her."

It was the one piece of her fantasies that she never got to see to the end. What did they do in the end? Did their friendship survive? Did it end and they became lovers? Did it all blow apart and they didn't even talk anymore? None of the options were great, but the last one was unacceptable under any circumstances. "That's not going to happen."

"How can you be so sure?"

"I'm…I'm not, but it can't. I won't let it." She groaned and covered her face with her hands, forgetting she was on video chat.

"See. That right there…" Cybil pointed her finger at her. "That's where you're wrong. I think you already know it's possible, otherwise it wouldn't be a big deal to do something other than see Maggie at the gym or for a meal. Those are safe, uncomplicated times you two spend together. Anything outside of that spells attraction. Involvement. The one thing you say you don't want, yet it's staring you right in the face." Cybil leaned in to drive home her point.

"Ugh. I hate you."

"You love me."

Rayne laughed. "You're right."

"Yes, I am, and that's why you have me sitting in ninety-plus degree weather at a shithole café where the only thing it has going for it is amazing coffee, so thanks for that." Cybil held up her mug and drank.

"Fine."

"Good. It's about time you admitted I'm right. Now, what kind of clothes are you going to buy?"

"I have no idea."

❖

Rayne gazed at her reflection. Her bra was loose around her though her breasts were still large. Her panties faded from black to just shy of gray. On the hook next to the mirror were three dresses, two pairs of slacks, and a few button-down blouses. She separated them into the categories of okay, nice, and hot. Whether that was how they were going to look on her was another matter. Maggie had tried to talk her into a few items that were meant for women who weren't afraid to flaunt their sexy bodies. Rayne wasn't that level of sexy. Sure, she was toned and had lost inches, dropping down a size or two, but that didn't mean she was going to make a spectacle of herself when she went out. Especially not when Maggie was going to tag along for "moral support and to keep the wrong type away." Whatever that meant.

She pulled a pair of navy polyester, straight-legged pants on and gave a satisfied nod when the hook and bar closure met without her having to suck in her stomach. The material pooled a little at her feet but felt good against her skin. The corresponding blouse was a bold geometric pattern, something she never would have picked for herself, but Maggie had insisted would accentuate her curves. Damn if she wasn't right. Rayne smoothed her hands over her hips and down her thighs. This wasn't a work outfit. This was a sophisticated look. Classy but not snobbish.

The dark tan linen ones fit as well as the first, and the cream, silk blouse with double fabric buttons at the cuffs made it dressier than the geometric one. The material also hinted at the color of her bra, and she liked it. She swapped out the pants for a chocolate brown pair of ankle ones with a three-inch slit accentuated by small black buttons. They were both casual and dressy. Maybe clothes shopping wasn't so bad after all.

"Rayne? Come out and let me see?" Maggie's voice traveled through the door.

"Why?" She did a slow spin, pausing for a few seconds to admire the shape of her ass. It wasn't the monster bubble she'd once thought.

"Because I want to see if my picks look good on you."

Rayne smoothed her hand down her thighs, then turned before she could change her mind. When she opened the door, Maggie was sitting on the bench with her forearms on her thighs. She glanced up and smiled.

"Very nice." Maggie sat back and her eyes traveled from Rayne's face down the full length of her body. "Turn for me."

It didn't occur to her until she was facing away that Maggie wanted the full effect and why that mattered didn't make any sense.

"Those look really good on you." Maggie's eyes held hers for a long time. "How about showing me something else?"

Pleasure coursed through her at Maggie's request. No one, not even Heather, had ever shown admiration for how she looked. Perhaps that had more to do with the type of clothes she used to wear most of the time, except for the occasions when Heather had a work event and Rayne begrudgingly put on one of her three or four outfits that were dressy enough. She wasn't going to waste her money on clothes, she only wore a few times a year. Maybe now she'd have a reason. "Sure."

"I can't wait."

Once she was securely behind the dressing room door, Rayne let out the breath she'd been holding. She slipped off the outfit, not bothering to put the items back on the hangers since they were definitely going home with her, then she stepped into one of the dresses she'd grabbed on a whim. The pattern of starbursts of white was subtle, but the background color was a vibrant shade of green. Somewhere between lime and that loud neon green that was popular at the moment. Before today she never would have thought to be so bold with her wardrobe, but she needed to get out of her former preference of staying in the background. Steve had said as much a few months ago, and his voice surfaced as she finished zipping.

"You're smart and talented, Rayne, but you're too quiet to be great. People build a reputation because they aren't shy about their abilities. Don't be shy, Rayne. Be bold."

The dress dipped at her cleavage. The tops of her breasts were visible, but not in a way that made her uncomfortable. The material clung in all the right places, accentuating her curves the way she liked. She wanted to know if Maggie would agree, and confidently stepped into the viewing area, but Maggie wasn't there. Now she felt foolish. Maggie hadn't waited around to see another outfit.

Rayne was about to retreat into the cubicle when Maggie's voice stopped her.

"Hey. I went to find another pair of slacks—"

Rayne turned to see what she was talking about. Maggie stood stunned. Her mouth was open, and she was definitely staring, but Rayne couldn't tell if it was in a good way, and her stomach dropped.

"Oh my God." Maggie's hands dropped and the pair of slacks dragged on the floor.

She wasn't sure she wanted to hear what Maggie was thinking. "What?" She glanced down at herself.

"That dress looks gorgeous on you," Maggie said before shaking her head. "No. You're gorgeous and the dress is a wonderful accessory."

Heat traveled up from her exposed chest to her ears and cheeks. She was going to die of embarrassment right there. Rayne broke eye contact. Absolutely she was going to die.

"I mean, you're always gorgeous, but wow, Rayne. Just… wow."

She should say something, right? Maggie had given her a big compliment and even though the rumor mill was rampant at the gym, she'd never heard Maggie be anything but professional with the members. "Thank you."

Maggie stepped closer. "No. Thank *you* for showing me. I can't wait to see the next one, too." She was intensely focused. Her eyes never wandered from Rayne's.

All she could do was nod. Her mind matched her insides. A big, jumbled ball of "What does that look mean?" Hadn't they just had this conversation at dinner a few days ago? When Maggie had been adamant they were building their friendship? If she was worried that getting involved wasn't in the cards, why would she start something fated to end in disaster? It made no sense. Ugh. And she needed to stop having expectations that were nothing more than fantasy. Rayne caught one last glance of herself before she whipped the dress off and put it on the pile to be purchased. The next dress she slipped over her head was one with three-quarter sleeves, an empire waist, and a crinoline-lined skirt. The color was deep purple with a tatted hemline, and the whole package made her feel like a princess. Only she wasn't waiting for her prince. Her prince was waiting for her. Rayne whispered to her reflection. "Stop. It's only because of the dream and it's time you let it go."

❖

Maggie lay awake, her mind a jumble of disconnected thoughts. She'd been working hard on her business plan, based on the grant writing handbook Rayne had brought her more than a week ago. There were instances when she got lost because the terms used were unfamiliar, but when she read it a second time, she was able to think in general terms rather than specifics. The aims and goals section had the universal language of how, when, and why with a projected outcome for her clients. Her target was a better overall feeling of well-being and inner harmony, the kind of calm and peace she could find in meditation, if only she could get out of her own head to be in the moment. The moments that were frequently present were the ones involving Rayne. It had been a battle of her will to not sweep Rayne up when they'd gone shopping. A woman of her caliber wouldn't be single for long. Maggie couldn't imagine Rayne not knowing how wonderful she was. Not only was she smart and funny, she was also beautiful. Just her luck the first person she had a profound interest in knowing intimately was becoming her best friend.

She hadn't had a friend like that since high school, and she and Aimee had lost touch after they left for college. Being on opposite coasts led to the eventual end of their robust friendship. A reason, a season, a lifetime. Such was the way of relationships in general. Hope for a long-term relationship, one that would survive for decades, had been in her heart once. Maggie wondered if she would ever have that feeling again.

Then Rayne came to the gym and a glimmer of hope had taken seed. What was it about Rayne that made Maggie take notice? It had to have been her energy. The aura of an internal force that surrounded her. There was no denying she was beautiful, but beautiful women were plentiful, and she'd always been content with no strings attached when it came to sleeping with women.

That wasn't the case with Rayne. In fact, Maggie had the feeling Rayne was exactly what she wanted in a partner and the reason she avoided that level of involvement. Rayne deserved a partner who was always present, not one who was stuck in the past. Yet, there was a thread of hope dangling in front of her that dared to be pulled. One that could end her loneliness and provide the kind of connection that only a partner...the right partner...can provide.

Maggie didn't consider herself a coward, and Rayne wasn't someone she could drop if things went sideways. Her insides were in turmoil, though she knew the only reasonable thing to do was be there for Rayne in the ways she needed. As a supportive, understanding friend who has vowed to do whatever she could to show Rayne she respected her and the goals she was working for. God help her.

Chapter Fourteen

It's been a pleasure, Ms. Flanders. I'm sorry we couldn't be more help." The bank officer shook her hand.

Shell-shocked and desperate, all Maggie could do was nod before walking though the lobby believing she'd run out of options. No one had shown any interest in the ad she'd placed seeking a business partner for her wellness center. Staffing wasn't the problem. She knew a lot of people who were capable of providing the types of services her place would offer. It was the capital investor she was lacking. Her dad had offered to "loan" her the start-up money, but she knew he'd never let her pay it back and she couldn't let herself rob her parents of the adventures her mom and dad had talked about doing when they retired. That day had come last year for her dad, approximately one year after her mother's retirement. Maggie was determined to find a way to open in the next twelve months if it was the last constructive thing she ever did.

Her biggest concern aside from the money was finding a place with ample parking. There was one other warehouse that might be doable. It was two blocks from the main road through town and in a mixed neighborhood of both residential houses and independent businesses. The attached lot could hold at least a dozen cars, maybe more. The one-story building had nine-foot ceilings and concrete floors. The industrial look was in so the HVAC system hanging from supports wouldn't be a problem, but the concrete floor was probably going to need to be revamped. The space had to be warm and inviting in the winter and cool and relaxing in the summer. Maybe the best solution would be heated flooring on top of the concrete.

The bank loan idea seemed reasonable at the time. There were a lot of programs out there for women, and she was sure the bank would have an inside line to the best ones, but like every other lead she'd discovered, the national economy was spiraling out of control and investment dollars had dried up. No one was willing to take a chance on a fledgling business, leaving her to wonder how any business got off the ground without having faith that it someday would be successful. Until that time came, Maggie was determined to keep searching for *her* someday.

"Fuck."

Maggie had run the numbers. A conservative estimate of mid-six figures would barely cover cosmetics and updates. Then there was the equipment, furniture, decorating, and at least a month of salary. It would take that long for word to get out they were open and what services they offered. An advertising campaign would cost another five thousand. Every time she thought of something else, the number grew. If she was serious about getting the name of her business out there, she needed a quarter of a million dollars.

"Double fuck."

The temptation to give up on her dream was ever present, but she wasn't a quitter. In her line of work, she constantly encouraged others to keep pushing, telling herself if she wanted it bad enough her dream would come true. It was time she heeded her own words and pushed forward. She had to believe she still had options and working on the details of the grant had refined some of her initial plans.

Once she was home and parked in the garage, she grabbed a container of leftover salad and stood at the kitchen sink, staring out the window at the flowers that were in bloom. Many of them needed her attention. Between the hours at the gym, the massages she did on the side, and the time she spent brainstorming, Maggie had sacrificed her time in the yard. There wasn't headspace for much more, but working outside gave her the calm she'd always found from tending to her plants and she needed to rely on that activity now as much as ever.

After tossing the container, Maggie headed for her bedroom. A quick shower before getting ready would help relieve some of the tension she was feeling. At least she had *something* to look forward to.

A little while later, Maggie fixed the knot of her tie loosely at her throat. The loud flowers on the soft silk from Thailand played off the dark maroon shirt she wore, made of the same material, along with the black slacks, were a classy combination. The person in the mirror wasn't handsome, but people had told her there was an enigmatic quality to her looks that drew people in. Of course, she wasn't naïve. Having a six-pack and impressive biceps didn't hurt either. And now she was off to help Rayne get back in the dating pool. There were times she'd called herself a fool in the past. This time she'd outdone herself. What had she been thinking?

Maggie parked in the driveway of a cute, well-kept one-story house. There were flowers in a small bed underneath a large, paned window and the warm light from inside spilled onto the walkway. The first and only time she'd previously been to Rayne's home had been to pick her up for a hike, and Rayne had met her on the walkway. Would she get a glimpse inside this time? She rang the bell, and the sound of wooden wind chimes made her smile. Rayne was anything but ordinary.

"Hi. I'm almost ready. Come in." Rayne stepped back. She wore a thick robe and had bare feet. Maggie didn't allow herself a chance to conjure if there was anything beneath the material.

"Thanks. I'm probably a little early. My Virgo personality dictates punctuality, which translates to being early or on time. Never late." She smiled as she talked. Her stomach tightened uncomfortably.

"Good to know. I tend to be late. Not because of my zodiac sign. I squirrel a lot." Rayne laughed. "Look around. Help yourself to a drink. I'll just be a few minutes." She disappeared down a short hallway, then closed the door to what Maggie assumed was her bedroom, but she wasn't going to follow that train of thought. Why had she agreed to go with Rayne to the monthly dance and social at the gay, queer, and everyone in between lounge?

She walked around the combination living/dining room slowly, taking in the things that revealed bits and pieces of Rayne's life. A small owl carved from a polished stone. Books on nature and wildlife. A safari picture of a smiling Rayne with another woman who might have been her best friend or a former lover. A sideboard with an impressive array of single-malt scotch and fine bourbons. She was tempted to pour an inch of amber into a tumbler but refrained. She was going to drive Rayne to the lounge from her place. She'd fixed a charcuterie board for later, unless Rayne took off with someone. The idea of someone else drawing Rayne's attention flared her protective instinct, which was ridiculous since she was the one who'd suggested Rayne "Get out among the masses." Whether her reaction was because of Rayne's reluctance or questioning her own motive she couldn't be sure. The clicking of heels on the hardwood floor brought her around to focus on Rayne's return.

"I think I'm overdressed." Rayne stood fussing with the hem of the knee-length portion of the beautiful dress she was wearing. The shiny aquamarine material with randomly spaced tiny white flowers played off the color of her blue-green eyes, reminding her of the hue of waters surrounding Greece. Along the edge of her lashes, a thin, black line ended in a short, upward sweep, drawing attention to not only the color but the shape of her eyes. Mascara and an enticing shade of plum lipstick defined her plump, kissable lips. Maggie had never seen Rayne in makeup, likely because Rayne didn't need makeup. Though she had to admit, it brought out her natural beauty.

"Wow."

Rayne's head shot up and she froze. "It's too much, isn't it?" The look on her face displayed defeat. "I'll go change."

"No." Maggie nearly shouted, startling Rayne. "Sorry. It's beautiful." She stepped closer and the scent of Rayne's perfume surrounded her like the steam from a hot tub that contained fragrant crystals. It was warm and inviting. "You look amazing." Her fingers twitched. She wanted to take Rayne's hand and…do what exactly she wasn't sure. It was the only reason she stood still. "I'm going to have to beat the women off with a big stick."

Rayne laughed. "I doubt that, but thank you for saying so." She gathered a small cross-body bag that matched her shiny black pumps and shawl. Then Rayne took a deep breath and smiled. "I think I'm ready." When Maggie didn't move, Rayne took a dangerously close step. "Maggie? Are you okay?"

She cleared her throat and shook off the cobwebs gathering in her brain. "Sure. Good to go." She hesitated, then bowed in a grand gesture. "May I escort you to the ball, ma' lady?"

"You most certainly may." Rayne slipped her arm through Maggie's at the elbow, and when their eyes met the sparkle in Rayne's made her more than a little sorry they weren't going as a couple.

Maggie glanced across the seat. Rayne stared out the side window and appeared lost in thought. Maybe she was having second thoughts about being seen with a player.

"If you'd rather do this alone, I'd understand."

Rayne blanched. "What? No." She reached across the short distance. "I'm really nervous and I'm really glad I'm not doing this alone." She gave a little squeeze, and Maggie's thigh tightened after she slid away.

Maggie took a silent, deep breath. She didn't want Rayne to see her nervous energy and why the rare affliction rose to the surface tonight was anyone's guess. Women were attractive. The ones who caught her attention most were the confident ones. The ones who knew what they wanted and how they wanted it. Rayne was not her usual fare. Rayne was unlike anyone Maggie had ever met and the most logical reason why Maggie was out of sorts. That, or she was coming down with a bug. She almost wished that was the cause of her insides tightening.

"I'm glad, too." Maggie pulled into a parking space and gave herself an abbreviated pep talk. She could do this. "Shall we go inside and show the women what they've been missing?" She was certain Rayne was going to balk or come up with a self-deprecating remark.

"Yes. I'm ready."

She nodded and pulled the key, then reached for the door. Rayne's fingers circled her forearm and a lightning rod shot directly to her clit, but she managed to look at Rayne.

"Thank you for this. For everything."

There was a finality to Rayne's words. As though this was the end, but of what, Maggie wasn't sure. "You're welcome." Now she had a new worry. Would she get through the night without making a complete fool of herself?

CHAPTER FIFTEEN

Rayne slowly emerged from the car, her mind a jumble of thoughts and images. When Maggie appeared at her door, there'd been a moment when her heart raced, but then reality crashed down on her and she remembered they weren't on a date, they were going out as friends. Maggie was just as striking in dress clothes as she was at the gym where there was little left to her imagination. Maggie met her at the front of the car.

"If you want to leave, let me know. I hope you enjoy the vibe." Maggie brushed a wayward curl from her eyes. "Ready?"

She wanted to say no, convinced heartbreak was inevitable, and she didn't want to hear the lies that would pave the way. But Maggie looked at her with such openness and her words were so encouraging, she swallowed the anxiety. "Yes."

Maggie nodded, then guided her to the door, her hand at the small of Rayne's back. The touch wasn't meant to be intimate. Rayne was sure of that. It felt like the most intimate touch ever though. Maggie reached around her to open the door and dance music greeted her. A song she liked to sing along with in the car welcomed her in and held the promise of a night to remember. Not because she was no longer hiding, but because she trusted Maggie would keep her from doing anything foolish. Maggie had her back in more ways than one, and she had to remember their friendship first. The disappointment wasn't new, but the intensity of it was unexpected.

"What do you want to drink?"

Rayne shivered. Maggie's lips were next to her ear. "What are you having?"

"Scotch. Single malt. Neat."

Maggie's breath was hot against her skin. "Would you please ask if they have any small batch bourbon?"

"They do." The look on her face must have shown her confusion. "Some nights I'm a switch hitter."

Wait. What?

"I have scotch when I'm driving because I drink slower." Maggie held up a finger, catching the bartender's attention. "Don't worry. I'll only have one or two. Do you want ice?"

"No. Thanks." She turned to the crowd, many of whom were on the dance floor. Others milled about in small groups, drinking and talking. A few were alone, like her, except she wasn't actually alone. The thumping rhythm awakened the former love she'd had for dancing. Heather hadn't appreciated the soulful, deep-reaching passion that music created for her and others. Unless, of course, she was trying to impress someone who could advance her career. She did whatever she had to do for the almighty dollar, and Rayne was glad Maggie wasn't interested in impressing anyone.

"Here you go." Maggie handed her the tumbler. "This is one of my favorites. I hope you like it."

"Thank you." She took a small sip. One time she'd made the mistake of taking a large gulp of a new liquor and the ensuing fire had scorched her throat. She must have coughed for a good twenty minutes. After that, she'd decided to test the waters before jumping in. The bourbon was deep and dark and smooth. It made her tongue tingle, but not in an unpleasant way. "It's very nice." In her opinion, the first sip of any drink was the best.

"Glad you approve." Maggie sipped from her tumbler and watched Rayne with focused attention. It made her uncomfortable and excited at the same time.

The focus needed to move away from her and on to the reason they were there. "How many of these events have you attended?"

Maggie tipped her head. "At least a couple a year. My schedule at the gym is hectic sometimes and with extra work and the time I spend on ways to get my own business up and running, there's not a lot of my free time for socializing."

She wasn't sure why Maggie might not consider their time together as part of her social life and it was disconcerting. Maybe they weren't as close as she thought. She should probably let it go, but she couldn't. "So our Friday night outings aren't social?"

"The time we spend together outside of the gym is more than social. It's what friends do." Maggie set her glass down, clearly done with the topic.

Rayne chastised her unreasonable reaction. Maggie had pointed out how much their relationship meant, just not the way Rayne had hoped. Would Maggie still be around if she could find the funds? How soon would that happen? Once she had what she needed, would Rayne lose the connection between them because she'd fall to the bottom of Maggie's priority list to concentrate on her business? Embarrassment coursed through her. Rayne's abandonment issues were hers to deal with, not Maggie's.

"What do you say we get out there and enjoy the vibes?" Maggie held out her hand.

Whatever reason she had for thinking Maggie was going to leave her in the lurch, it had to stop. "You might think otherwise once you've seen me dance." She chuckled.

"I doubt that. Besides..." Maggie winked. "I might be the one with two left feet."

There wasn't one thing she'd ever seen Maggie attempt that she didn't master. The woman had moves. Whether they carried over to the dance floor was one more thing Rayne was about to find out. "Only one way to be sure." She took a bigger sip and hoped it relaxed her enough so she didn't make a spectacle. Somehow, she had the feeling Maggie wouldn't care, and that was a good thing.

Rayne washed her hands in the restroom and dabbed sweat from her face, careful not to ruin her makeup. The alcohol was just enough that when a fast, familiar dance tune played, Rayne was able to find her rhythm. Maggie stayed close, but not close enough to ward off any potentially interested woman, though she didn't have her hopes set on that happening. She looked good in the dress she'd bought on her own as a surprise for Maggie. And she was having fun despite the nerves that had persisted through the first dozen songs.

Allowing herself to let go hadn't been easy after years of being on her best behavior whenever she accompanied Heather on a work event. Rigid work protocols added to the regimen she'd fallen into, a routine that had proven to provide results both in and out of the lab. The part that was missing was having fun. Until recently—until Maggie—she hadn't been having fun in either. The bigger question was when had that happened and how had she let it slip away?

Work used to hold a particular type of joy. Discovery of a new bit of information or validation of a theory that up until that moment had only been a possible solution but hadn't been based on proven fact. That was exciting. That's what she loved about science. That joy had slowly seeped away while she moved through day-to-day life. That wasn't living, it was existing. Maggie had helped her see that, and tonight was just one more example of staying in the moment instead of ignoring what was right in front of her. She opened the door and went in search of Maggie, determined to show her how much she appreciated tonight, and to tell her how much fun she was having. There was also something nagging in the back of her mind. She was sure it was important, otherwise why was it there? It probably had to do with work, and she'd promised Maggie she'd give her brain a rest for tonight.

"Hey, gorgeous. Are you having a good time?" A woman with blue tint at the tips of her blond, spiked hair leaned against the wall, a beer bottle dangling from her fingertips. She had a nice smile. Rayne didn't want to seem too interested even though she was supposed to be exploring her options, putting herself out there and seeing where things led, if anywhere.

"Hi. I am." She shoved her hands in her dress pockets, glad not for the first time, for the option. "How about you?"

"I could tell you were by the way you were dancing. You've got good rhythm."

Rayne felt the flush heat her cheeks. She hated when it happened and wished there was a way to stop it. Maybe the lights were low enough not to be noticed. "Thanks." She searched for something else to say. "You didn't answer my question."

"You're right." The woman finished her beer and set the empty on a nearby table. "My night could be better." One brow rose and she stuck out her hand. "I'm Terry."

Not a neanderthal after all. "Nice to meet you. I'm Rayne."

"As in pouring down buckets?" Terry smiled and tipped her head to one side.

"No. R-A-Y-N-E."

"Unusual, but nice."

"Thanks. I think." Was she flirting? Could she do this? Rayne glanced at the crowd. It didn't take her long to find Maggie standing at the bar, watching her. She tried to decipher what Maggie was thinking when she raised her glass and nodded. Maybe she smiled, too. It was hard to tell this far away. She should think about having her eyes checked again. There were a pair of glasses on her desk at work, but they were only magnifying lenses. It was possible that she needed more help seeing by now.

"Is that your girlfriend?" Terry asked.

She snapped her head around. "What? No. She's a good friend. She's the one who talked me into coming out tonight." Rayne was babbling. This was why she'd never been good at dating. Women who paid attention to her made her nervous.

"Congratulations on coming out. Would you like a drink to celebrate?" Terry's smirk wasn't unkind, but she wasn't in the mood for jokes either. "Sorry." Terry apologized like she meant it. "My timing sucks sometimes."

Rayne didn't want to be hit on. She didn't want to have meaningless conversations with strangers, even the ones who were easy on the eyes. "It was nice to meet you, but I think I'm going to call it a night."

"Sure. Another time maybe."

"Maybe." She started to turn away. When had she become so rude. The woman wasn't being cocky or all touchy-feely. She appeared to be interested. "I'm sorry. It's the first time I've been out since my breakup and I'm a lot out of practice."

Terry held up her hands in surrender. "Say no more. I get it. I never could resist a beautiful woman. Have a good night, Rayne, and just for the record, you did fine." Terry moved into the mass of people.

Relief flooded in at the same time she regretted not being able to just let go. Have fun. That's why she was there wasn't it?

❖

Maggie finished her drink, studying Rayne. "I thought for a minute you were going to get some action." She smiled through the flare of jealousy that needed tamping down. She couldn't be upset with Rayne for talking to women, even if it was only one.

"That was Terry." Rayne ordered a seltzer with a twist.

"You know her?" There wasn't any way to keep the surprise out of her voice.

"I do now." Rayne laughed and her angst about running into someone she knew dissipated.

"You could have hung out. I'm fine." She wasn't fine though. The mama bear instinct ran just below the surface. She didn't want anyone taking advantage of Rayne. Heather had done that, and it had taken Rayne months to recover.

Rayne's gaze softened. "That's sweet of you, but I think I'm ready to go."

"Are you sure?"

Rayne glanced around at the dance floor. Some people were laughing as they talked and shared a funny story; others were clearly ready to make out. "I'm sure." Rayne opened her bag and fished out her credit card.

"Uh-uh. This is on me." She handed her bank card to a bartender and pulled a twenty from a small stack of bills.

"Can't I at least split it with you?"

"Nope." She scribbled her signature on the line and tucked her card away. "Maybe next time." She guided Maggie past a new group of twenty-somethings and out into the warm night air. Despite being fully aware she should leave it alone, she couldn't. "So, initial thoughts?" She opened the passenger side door. Once Rayne was in, she took a breath. As she rounded to her side, she took a deeper breath. *This was not a date. Rayne is not my girlfriend.* Simple enough. Nothing was that simple. Not getting the backing to open her business. Not telling herself she was happy with her life. Not the idea of her and Rayne keeping to the only friends rule. Not one damn thing was simple right now.

"I'm starving," Rayne said.

Maggie took another breath. "I've got food." This was a bad idea. "And alcohol."

Rayne laughed. "Okay, then." Rayne was smiling as she watched the darkness slide by.

Maggie made up her mind in those few seconds that being a player had been her safety net and now all she wanted to do was fall.

CHAPTER SIXTEEN

There're not any options left." Maggie chewed her tasteless salad.

"What about the grant you mentioned? Isn't the government providing women start-up money for entrepreneurs?" Larry was deep in thought, bless his soul.

"They are, but the competition is fierce, and even with generous projections, there's a fifty-fifty chance a new business will fail in the first three years." After completing the rough draft, Rayne had read her grant proposal and made annotations where she thought more or less details were needed. She explained that applications failed most often due to a lack of understanding of the underlying goals of the project, which were crucial to obtaining funding. "The Feds want a sure bet, and I don't think that's possible in today's climate for most start-ups." Maggie had done her best to come up with a solid plan and ideas on how to circumvent any foreseeable obstacles. She was no closer to her dream today than she was six months ago. About the same time she met Rayne.

"That really sucks." Larry patted her on the back and went to go check supplies in the locker room.

Maggie pulled her hands down her face. Defeat wasn't familiar to her, and she hated the way it weighed on her. There had to be an answer.

"A dollar for your thoughts."

Her smile came naturally. "A dollar?" Maggie turned to see Rayne's sweet smile shining back at her.

"Inflation. What's got you looking so worried?" Rayne smoothed the spot between her brows.

It didn't mean anything aside from a friend showing concern, but inside Maggie's neuron-overloaded brain it felt like much more. They'd been settled into a comfortable place since a few weeks ago when Maggie's unwarranted jealous streak had shown up the night of the dance. She'd impressed Rayne with the charcuterie board and the fruity bottle of white they shared. The conversation was light but thoughtful, too. When Rayne left almost two hours later, Maggie was able to compartmentalize her irrational reaction as concern about Rayne and not wanting her to fall prey to a stranger. But Rayne had been absent from both the gym and their meet-up during the last week because of experiments at work. She didn't realize how much she missed her until this minute.

"Hey, stranger. How has work been?"

"Don't deflect."

Maggie chuckled. "Same old story with trying to find backing for the business." Even with Rayne's help it felt like she didn't have much choice but to let the dream die a slow and painful death. She glanced around the gym and saw a number of familiar faces. Disliking her job wasn't an issue. Helping people obtain results was what she did, and she did it well.

Rayne nodded. "We should talk. I have another idea."

As much as she knew Rayne wanted to alleviate her disappointment, she wasn't sure how much she wanted Rayne involved in bringing her aspiration to fruition, but spending time with Rayne would be a nice diversion from being stuck in her own head. "Okay. What do you have in mind?"

Rayne tapped her chin. "I'll text you." She glanced at the clock. "I better get my ass in gear, or my trainer will have me doing some crazy routine because I've been MIA." She sauntered to the water fountain, filled her water bottle, then grabbed a towel from the stack. On her way by, she smacked Maggie on the ass as she uttered, "Later."

Her mouth hung open. Rayne never engaged in casual touches. Twice in one day had her questioning if that was what Rayne wanted to discuss. She'd been pushing her own thoughts of involvement away, telling herself just because a part of her hoped Rayne found her interesting and fun, there might be a slight possibility that it wasn't all friendship. That was crazy. Right? Maggie hadn't considered wanting a romantic relationship in years. Was that because she couldn't stand the thought of losing love for a shitty reason, or because she hadn't met anyone that moved her in that direction. She rubbed the spot that Rayne had smacked and smiled at the lingering tingle, all the while hoping Rayne didn't keep her wondering too long regarding what she wanted to talk about.

Did I really do that? Rayne had five minutes left on the elliptical and her thoughts wandered to the earlier conversation with Maggie. What had she been thinking when she slapped Maggie's ass? Granted, it was a nice ass but still, that was so not like her. Maybe it had something to do with the recurring dream. She thought Maggie's nighttime appearance was gone from her sleeping self for good. Then last week, it came back with a vengeance and was on repeat most nights since then. No matter what she tried, nothing chased away the visions. Her only option was to enjoy it, waking up wet and wanting whenever it happened. It wasn't a horrible outcome, but being frustrated over and over again wasn't great either. Maybe the slap had been an unconscious need to actually feel the ass that at one point in the fantasy she'd gotten to hang on to.

She hadn't lied to Maggie about having an idea that had nothing to do with her sleeping fantasies. In the wake of looking for grants she could apply for, she'd come across one for incubator companies addressing climate change related health concerns. She had a good basic idea of Maggie's venture, but if they addressed the physical and mental issues that weather and natural disasters had on people, applying was worth a shot. Before they met though, she needed to have an outline of the questions this specific grant was looking for and how the business would address them. For that reason, she was going to need a couple of days. After she had the basics down, she'd confirm with Maggie, and together they could work on the new application that she hoped would be hard to ignore. That is, if Maggie wanted to spend the additional hours with her.

Now that she'd reached her goal of losing some weight and getting into better physical shape, she no longer needed one-on-one training and she'd stopped paying for personal training sessions several months ago. Since that time, their friendship had grown and a weekly meal or two was the way they kept in touch with each other. In hindsight, she wasn't sure she knew all that much about Maggie's personal life aside from knowing where she grew up, that she had a brother who was a storm chaser, and that while her parents weren't wealthy, they had been able to give their children a secure upbringing without financial worries.

Comparing what she knew about Maggie to what she knew about her best friend Cybil, Rayne realized there was a huge gulf between her knowledge base with Maggie, and she wanted that to change. Granted, it had taken years to form the depth of friendship she had with Cybil, but she might not have years to form that kind of a bond with Maggie, and she wanted to. If she helped Maggie get the grant, was she also giving her an escape route to spending less time together?

Rayne slowed the machine and drank room temperature water. She wasn't a selfish person. If Maggie's dream became a reality, with or without her help, she'd be happy for her. It was the right reaction for a friend to have, and she wanted to be that friend. A little part of her though, would be sad. The same thing could be said about her own dream. Someday she'd have a lab of her own. It was the coveted benchmark of success in the world of science. The normal progress of dedication. Graduate student, to postdoctoral fellow, to being funded and opening her own laboratory as a principal investigator.

So what if she had to sacrifice a personal life for her career. She sucked in a quick breath. That's what Heather had done. She'd chosen her career over a relationship in search of the brass ring. What did that say about Rayne? She shook her head. She wasn't Heather and there was no lover, or love, in her life to choose one over the other. That was a good thing. What more could she ask for?

CHAPTER SEVENTEEN

So you really think I have a shot?" Maggie asked.

Rayne chewed while formulating an answer that was honest. "Yes, and tackling this together is the best approach." She put down her fork and picked up her margarita. "Don't be upset. If there's one thing I've learned, it's how to write a grant in a way that will get the funding entity to take notice, and that's what you need, an edge above the competition."

Maggie's mouth moved into something between a smile and a smirk. "And you're my edge?"

The laugh was meant to keep her from being too serious. Writing grants was serious business, but she didn't want the experience to lack fun. "We can make a proposal that will address some of the underlying contributing factors to health concerns related to climate change." She drained her glass. "Of course, I'll have to know more about the details and structure of the business, the financial implications and requirements, staffing, etcetera. You know, the nuts and bolts of your plan."

"Nuts and bolts, huh?" Maggie studied her and it was hard to discern what was behind the penetrating gaze.

"What I read in your draft was a promising start, but it needs to be specific to this funding line. That's more critical with this money source than a general fund grant might be." A disturbing thought crossed her mind. "Please tell me you have more details in mind."

Maggie let out a full and hearty laugh. "I damn well better develop them if I don't."

She reached out to touch Maggie's hand. "Hey, I didn't mean to offend you."

"Sorry. I'm frustrated over the whole thing and I'm close to my breaking point. It's about time I face reality."

"Don't say that. You can do this."

"Oh, so now it's back on me?"

Rayne slapped Maggie's hand.

"Ow."

"I hardly touched you." She tipped her head at the waiter and pointed to their glasses to indicate another round of drinks was in order. "Since when are you a wimp?"

"Since you've developed some serious muscles." Maggie picked up her glass to finish hers, too, then moved it to the edge of the table next to Rayne's.

"I had a great trainer. Even if she was a hard-ass at times."

"Huh. I thought you liked my hard ass." Maggie chuckled. The waiter replaced their empty glasses with fresh drinks then disappeared. "To hard asses."

Reluctantly, she remembered smacking her before she touched her glass to Maggie's. The sound was soft, but the ring reminded her of another toast from not too long ago when she'd agreed to friendship after mentioning her dream offhandedly. She glanced down at her half-eaten plate. She shouldn't make promises she might not be able to keep.

"What are you thinking about?"

She had to come up with something quick. "Between the water and the drinks, I think I might explode." Nothing sexy in that statement. "I'll be right back." Rayne smiled, not wanting Maggie to think there was a problem, because there wasn't.

"Okay."

Rayne felt eyes on her as she made her way to the door that said "Senoritas" on it. Once she was safely locked inside a stall, she lowered her pants and dropped onto the seat and held her face in her hands. She was about to suggest they spend an inordinate amount of time together to work on a proposal that would up the odds of Maggie getting an award. Was that what she wanted to do considering all she could think about was Maggie's ass along with the rest of her muscular body? She let out a sigh and finished up. She studied her reflection as she washed her hands. As Maggie's friend, there was no doubt she wanted to help. There was another part of her though that poked and prodded for more. "Stop." Rayne silently mouthed the word.

She emerged to find Maggie sitting back, relaxed and slowly licking salt off the rim of her glass between sips. Rayne took a deep breath and sat down. The rest of the night would be awkward if she let it.

"Feel better?"

"Much. Thanks."

"But that's not the reason you escaped to the bathroom. Again."

It was clear Maggie wasn't going to be put off so easily this time, and she finally managed to meet Maggie's gaze. "It's back."

"What's back?" Maggie grabbed a tortilla chip and dipped it into the never-ending bowl of salsa.

Since she started the topic change, she might as well keep going. "The dream."

Maggie looked thoroughly confused. "What dream?"

Rayne shifted restlessly before leaning in. "Remember a few weeks ago you wanted to know why I looked tired?"

"Sure."

"And I told you it was nothing, just a dream."

"It didn't seem like a big deal." Maggie scooped up salsa with her chip and crunched.

"Yes, well, it was more than that because you were in it."

"Oh, really? Was I being a hard-ass trainer?" Maggie chuckled.

"Not exactly. You…and I…" She swallowed around the words. "Well, we were in bed."

"Oh, shit," she said as her eyes got big. "A sex dream?"

"I'm going to die." She covered her face as heat rose up her neck.

Maggie laughed and tried to pull her hands away. "You're not going to die, silly."

"I might."

"Then who's going to write the grant that's going to get me a shitload of money?"

Rayne let her hands drop to her lap. "Good point." She drank, then snagged a chip.

"So, there's no harm in telling me the details." Maggie's brows rose and fell several times. "Was it good? Was I good?"

Now she really was going to die.

"Ooh, maybe it was you doing the fun stuff. There had to be fun stuff. I like…" Maggie glanced around and moved closer. "I like sex to be a fun time on occasion, you know? In between the hot and steamy stuff."

"Please, Maggie. Please stop." What she saw in Maggie's gaze stole her breath and the rest of the world faded away. If she didn't know better, she'd describe it as desire, but that was crazy thinking.

"Is that what you said? Did you beg me to stop?"

"Oh, God. No, no. You…I…the dream was interrupted."

"Damn. That's wrong on so many levels."

Rayne mumbled under her breath. "Tell me about it."

"It's something I've thought about," Maggie said quietly. "I didn't tell you because I was afraid you'd turn me away. More afraid it would ruin our friendship after I'd insisted our friendship came first."

News alert. Rayne's heart thudded so hard and loud Maggie had to see it or hear it. The idea that she had even considered being with her outside of their friendship—or was that inside of their friendship—threw a wrench in all her preconceived reasons for not telling Maggie about her attraction. She never would have guessed Mags was the least bit attracted to her. Not in a million years. Had she missed some sign? Some indication of wanting more than friendship? Rayne didn't think so, but then she also had no clue Maggie would confess to having thoughts of taking what they shared to another level.

The alcohol Rayne drank was like truth serum and she was about to spill her guts. "I would have never guessed." Screenshots of their times together flashed through her mind. There wasn't one instance she could point to that would indicate Maggie thought about her the same way she thought about Maggie.

Maggie sighed heavily. "It's discouraged by my employer. We're supposed to maintain a 'professional distance' at all times from the clientele."

"Has that ever stopped you?" The rumor mill was rampant at the gym, and she wanted to know if the scuttlebutt was true.

"I wish I could say yes, but I'm sure you've heard people talking."

Rayne nodded. "I don't pay much attention." She hadn't. Not really. Those women weren't friends with Maggie, and she'd given her the benefit of the doubt, though now she wondered how much of it was true.

"Like I said, I wasn't sure how you'd respond." Maggie folded her hands on the table. "I'm not sure if I'll ever be ready for an intimate relationship."

Rayne was reeling from her own confession and now there was Maggie's to consider. It was too much to think about. There was so much she wanted to ask, though she wasn't sure she was ready to hear things she may not want to know about hanging in the air. "I know we should talk more about our confessions, but right now I'd like to finish dinner and relax." She saw the relief wash over Maggie's strained features. "I hope you don't mind."

"I think that's a marvelous idea." Maggie picked up her glass, licked the rim, then sipped. "Would you like another?" she asked.

Rayne hadn't realized she'd drained the contents of her drink but was sure it would hit her shortly. She shook her head. "You could have told me to slow down." She pointed to the condensation-covered glass.

"And ruin all your fun? I'd never want to do that."

The waiter removed her dish after she indicated she couldn't eat any more. She'd been ravenous, and she wasn't the only one. Maggie had all but cleaned her plate.

"Would you like coffee? Dessert?" the waiter asked.

Maggie wiped her mouth, then swallowed the last of her drink. "Definitely coffee, but I'll wait on dessert."

The idea of a hot cup of coffee sounded good and Rayne nodded in agreement. Most of the time, she enjoyed prolonging their evenings together. Tonight, all she wanted to do was get out of there and hide under the covers. She'd revealed too much. Said too much. And Maggie was going to be seeing a lot more of her if she accepted her offer to help with the new grant. She was the one who needed help now.

❖

Standing in line was one of the few things that tried Rayne's patience. She wasn't sure why, but even if she knew she was certain it wouldn't help.

"When you're desperate for coffee the line moves at a snail's pace."

Rayne smiled. The woman's voice had a pleasant timbre, and curiosity caused her to look over her shoulder. The woman smiled and her eyes were mischievous. Not wanting to be rude, she joined in. "What's the longest you've ever waited before giving up?"

The woman wore a linen suitcoat over a turtleneck sweater and sharply creased black jeans. Her hair was styled to look like she'd just gotten out of bed, and she had the type of blue eyes that were easy to get lost in. "I never give up."

"That's impressive."

"Not really. Once I've committed to something I see it through."

Rayne could appreciate that mentality. She was the same way when it came to her research, though lately it was more of a struggle than she wanted to admit. Even if things didn't go according to how she hypothesized, she managed to see it through to the end. That's what she hoped to talk with Maggie about, too. She'd been on pins and needles since dinner the other night. Unfortunately, the discussion would have to wait with a twelve-hour experiment ahead, and a long day to follow, there was no time for a heart-to-heart. Now she understood the meaning behind the sentiment.

"I'm Fran," she said, holding out her hand.

She hesitated. "I'm Rayne." They shook with just the right amount of firmness. Thankfully, Fran's palm was dry. A sweaty palm always made her feel icky.

"It's nice to meet a fellow sufferer."

Rayne tipped her head.

"We still don't have coffee."

She laughed. "True, but we're closer to the finish line."

"I like your optimism. Is it inherent or learned?"

When the person in front of her moved forward so did she. She wasn't sure how to take the flirtatious way the Fran leaned in. There wasn't a plausible reason for her discomfort, but it was plain that's how she felt. "I like to think it's inherent." While there were a number of traits she could attribute to her parents she was more apt to believe this one was hers to claim.

"Nice."

Another step. There were only two people ahead of her now.

"Would you like to do this again sometime?"

Rayne half turned. "Stand in line?"

"As much as I've enjoyed standing in this one, I meant go for coffee together sometime."

There was only one person she wanted to make plans with. "I'm sorry, but no."

Fran's surprise showed on her face. "My apology. I thought…" Fran sighed and shook her head. "My mistake." Fran pointed. "You're up."

"Next." The barista called out, looking like she wanted to be somewhere else. Rayne suddenly felt the same way.

"Hi." She gave her order and paid, then moved to the end of the counter, knowing it could be another ten minutes until she actually had her drink. When it was less than five, she couldn't help being happy. "Thank you." She glanced at her watch, then at Fran. "I've got to run. Enjoy your coffee."

"You, too."

Rayne hustled out the door. The idea of dating might be fun if circumstances were different, but she had no interest in testing the waters. If she did, it would be with the woman in her dream. At least she could enjoy the fantasy of Maggie being in her bed, even if it never happened for real. Then why was she so sad?

CHAPTER EIGHTEEN

Maggie's heart thumped in her chest the same as it had during the entire dinner with Rayne. She hadn't missed the flush that rose over the top of Rayne's V-neck top and continued along her supple-looking throat before landing on her cheeks. That was right after Rayne mentioned the dream was back. Why she'd picked that night, at a restaurant no less, to confess her true feelings for Rayne was a mystery. Knowing Rayne had been having sexual dreams about her was shocking and felt good at the same time and had given her courage to convey her own imaginings. Maybe that was part of the reason she would sometimes find Rayne creating space between them or glancing at her sideways.

They'd had fun after the awkward moments immediately following Rayne's nature of the dream as erotic. At least, that's where Maggie's mind went even though Rayne hadn't elaborated, and truth be told, she wasn't sure she wanted to hear the details. Not in public anyway. If they were going to have a conversation like that, it had to be somewhere private because Maggie wasn't sure how Rayne felt about the implications or what her own reaction would be, and she didn't want Rayne to be embarrassed like that. Honestly though, she wouldn't mind hearing what the dream had entailed.

Not long after Rayne had hired her as a trainer, Maggie had begun to have a deeper appreciation of the woman behind the insecurities. The same could not be said for her previous liaisons.

They had been mostly pleasant distractions—necessary physical interactions, so unlike the much deeper, distinct type of relationship she had found with Eve. She'd begun to to have those intimate wonderings about Rayne. The one person she was most afraid to become more involved with.

She'd been single so long, and her priorities had changed on an epic scale once she accepted Eve's death. She no longer blamed herself for missing a warning sign that would have gotten her help, or to the doctor. Something. Anything. Acknowledging that she could move on without worrying over how to handle the lingering guilt was a priority. There were a few people she no longer had to answer to, like Eve's parents. They might not have blamed her in so many words but it was clearly written on their faces. The judgmental people around her didn't contribute to her joy, or the elation her accomplishments brought. She had to remember she was no longer stuck in time.

That was then and this was now. Her new plans included more of doing what she loved by helping as many people as possible in her own way. Those plans had been moved to the forefront while she enjoyed working at the gym and doing independent massages for affluent clients. Someday, she'd have it all. Until then, she was going to enjoy life and make a point of having fun.

Maggie wanted to know where Rayne's head was. She needed to make sure things between them were still good. Having sex, even if in a dream, could make things wonky, and she hated the idea they'd no longer be friends, or worse, become estranged. If that happened they might as well sleep together and enjoy the stroke of fate that brought them together. Because Maggie believed in fate, which was what brought her out of the most difficult time of her life. Dealing with Eve's death was the hardest thing she'd ever faced, and she didn't want Rayne to have to go through any more pain than she already had either. It didn't matter that the comparison with a breakup couldn't equal the death of a partner. Who was she to judge? Rayne had been timid and lacked any confidence when she came to the gym. Everyone grieved loss differently. She didn't want their time together to be spent worrying about what ifs. And she wouldn't know if she didn't ask, even if her heart was telling her to not shut the door on love.

❖

"Hello?" Rayne's voice was heavy with sleep. Calling at this hour was a bad idea.

"Hi."

"Hey, Maggie, are you okay?" She could hear the sound of Rayne rustling her bedding.

"Uh…yeah. Sorry to be calling so late." Maggie paced the length of the kitchen.

"It's fine. Really." Rayne sounded wide awake.

"Can I come over? We need to talk." She was a bit hesitant, but she really wanted to see Rayne. The flirty comments during dinner hadn't helped ease her mind about where they stood, and she didn't want Rayne to get the wrong impression. She might be a player, but she wasn't going to treat Rayne like she treated the others from the gym. Rayne was special. Dating wasn't totally out of the question, but she wanted to be mindful of Rayne's reputation as a client, even if that client had become a really good friend in the process. She was glad she helped Rayne find confidence in her abilities in the gym, but that's where her professional obligation ended.

She didn't want to jump to conclusions either. Rayne might have been embarrassed by her dream, but that could be for any number of reasons. Maggie had to be sure before she did irreparable damage to their friendship by assuming Rayne was interested in pursuing a deeper relationship. Well, maybe not pursue, but Rayne had been uncomfortable enough to avoid the topic for the rest of the evening. That left Maggie wondering if there was a reason *she* was freaking out, or if her head was too big and Rayne didn't want to hurt her feelings by telling her no way, no how. Little did Rayne know she'd almost be happy with being told she wasn't interested. It wouldn't feel right to use their friendship as leverage for feeling obligated. When the time came and she found an investor, or the grant Rayne was confident that between the two of them would be awarded, it would make a good impression with a future partner. She wanted to be able to trust that Rayne would understand her having limited time for a relationship. Maggie was looking forward to being devoted to setting up the business.

"Maggie? You still there?"

Fuck! "Yeah, I'm here."

"Come on over. I'll put some coffee on."

"Okay. Be there in a few." A moment of silence compounded her awkward feelings. "Rayne?"

"Hmm?"

"Thanks."

"You're welcome. Now move your ass before I fall back to sleep."

Maggie giggled and disconnected. She pictured Rayne in her kitchen where she appeared a lot more at home than Maggie did. Except for special occasions. She loved planning birthday parties, or events like when her friend graduated with her PhD. Or when her roommate got engaged there was that fun bash at the park in the middle of a rainstorm and no one cared about getting wet. It was a beastly summer afternoon, and the downpour was a welcome guest. She danced barefoot in the grass with a bottle of beer as her partner. Everyone there was smiling and laughing at her antics. Eve had arrived late like she always did, but she jumped right in among the revelers. When the storm passed, Eve went to her car and pulled out stacks of towels.

"I thought you might want these at some point." Eve handed one to each person and stacked the surplus on a dry corner of the table. That's how she was. That's *who* she was.

Her head spun. Caught between the past and present along with her plans for the future, Maggie wondered where Rayne might fit in. It made her stomach hurt. *What the hell am I doing?* Maggie stared out the windshield to get her bearings. This wasn't college. She wasn't in love, but damn, the comparison to the only person she had loved was similar.

Maggie parked by the all-night bakery, the only storefront with lights on, and got out. Resolve coursed through her. Rayne was a sweetheart and a good person. Maggie wanted to make sure there were no promises she couldn't keep. No grand gesture of a happily ever after if there wasn't an understanding between them. It might take more than a late-night conversation to sort it all out, but that's what she had to do. There were no other feasible options. If the conversation didn't go as planned, Rayne would find someone who could complement her. And Maggie…Maggie would continue on her mission that included financial independence and casual fucks without emotional involvement. She'd managed this long, and she could continue to do so. Then why did the sound of it feel so wrong?

CHAPTER NINETEEN

"Hey," Maggie said a little too enthusiastically. Maybe she was more nervous than she realized.

"You're awfully chipper for the middle of the night."

Rayne looked fantastic, even at this hour. She wore a pair of dark leggings and a comfortable-looking oversized oxford shirt. Her feet were bare, and her hair was tousled in that just-out-of-bed way that made her wish she was the reason for how it looked.

"Sorry." She cast her gaze to the ground, not wanting Rayne to see the inner turmoil.

"Don't be sorry. I think it's funny." Rayne stepped back and waved her inside.

"You mentioned coffee, so I made a pit stop at a bakery. I hope that's okay?" she said almost apologetically. Rayne leaned against the closed door, looking a little sleepy, a little curious, and a whole lot sexy. *Seriously, dude? Do not go there.*

"Really? There's an all-night one?" Rayne's eyes narrowed. "Is this some underhanded move to make me feel guilty so I agree to more hikes?"

Stricken for a second, Maggie almost vehemently denied the assumption, but Rayne was smiling that cute, "I made a funny," look and she laughed in spite of her nerves. Against her better judgment, she moved closer to Rayne.

"You never have to feel guilty about not doing something you don't enjoy, Rayne. Not ever. Not with me." Her breathing shifted and her gaze went to Rayne's pouty mouth and glistening lips. Did she have lip gloss on? What flavor was she wearing? She imagined swiping her tongue over the surface, feeling the softness, memorizing the taste of them.

Rayne's chest rose and fell quickly. Her gaze met Maggie's. "What's in the bag?"

"Something decadent…" She paused for a beat. "And sweet. To share." Her mouth twitched. What the hell was she doing? Hadn't she just had a talk with herself about making sure Rayne was on the same page? Christ.

"Then I better check the coffee." Rayne slid away and she was left staring at the backside of her retreating figure.

Try as she might to ignore the flutter in her lower belly, Maggie couldn't deny it was there. It blossomed and grew with each passing second. The idea she was the only one having this reaction was like a bucket of cold water. Quickly on the heel of that singular thought was the one of Rayne playing with her. The gym was full of whispers, and some had to do with her conquests. It left a bad taste in her mouth. She had to say something.

"Rayne?"

"Hmm?"

When she didn't continue, Rayne turned. "Whatever you've heard about me, most of it isn't true." She swallowed. This was proving harder than she thought.

"Most?" Rayne cocked her hip against the counter. She'd look so good sitting on it with her legs spread, waiting. "What do you think I've heard, Mags?" The pulse in Rayne's neck visibly throbbed.

The gush of excitement caused her to make a sound. Some pathetic, needy little moan-gasp thing that she couldn't hide and didn't want to. "That I…" She broke eye contact and glanced at the floor. "I'm not sure. I'm your friend and I don't want that to change."

Rayne appeared to consider it. "Neither do I, but if I didn't know better, Mags, I'd say you were flirting with me a few minutes ago." Rayne moved to go around her, but Maggie stepped into her path, leaving the barest bit of space between them. If Rayne moved, they'd brush against each other.

"Would that be a bad thing?" For an instant, Rayne's gaze flicked to her lips. Why was she doing this? Why was she pretending she wasn't attracted to Rayne when there were times she couldn't stop thinking about her? She really, really had to stop, though. She had to take control before things spiraled into something primal without any thought of the implications, or the possibility she'd give in and there'd be an awkward morning after.

Rayne's lips pursed and she took a deep breath. "You tell me."

When Maggie couldn't think of a single thing to say, Rayne turned to the counter and Maggie stepped closer. She was doing a pretty good job of making a mess of the situation. For the first time, she noticed the table was already set with napkins, mugs, spoons, sugar, and cream. "Can I help?"

"Yes, you can. First, you need to give me space. Okay? Having you get close is confusing and distracting."

Maggie backed away a few steps. The kitchen wasn't huge, but it was better than nothing. With the safety of a little distance between them, she added the bakery bag to the mix while counting to ten.

"There's small plates in the upper cupboard next to the stove hood." Rayne pointed to her left before retrieving the coffee carafe.

In the silence, Maggie had a momentary degree of sanity. That was good. This was serious. Not life-or-death serious, but if they couldn't resolve the discomfort between them, well, at least hers, there might not be any coming back from all the angst and conflicting thoughts. She hummed as she carried out her assigned task. Rayne didn't make eye contact. Maybe she couldn't. Perhaps she'd sent one too many mixed messages. Hell, she was the one sending them, and was dumbfounded by her own actions. This night might well end on a sour note. It wasn't like it wasn't a real possibility. Dream or not, Rayne might not have had any sexual or romantic thoughts about her. As deflating as the idea was, it *was* what she wanted. Wasn't it?

Chapter Twenty

Rayne hadn't had much time to consider how she felt about Mags as someone other than her friend, or what that implied. Of course, she was a handsome, masc-presenting woman, and those were the physical descriptors she fantasized about in a partner. Being smart, funny, capable, and independent were characteristics that would sustain a relationship, and Maggie had those, too. She wasn't intimidated by anyone as far as Rayne could tell. Many of the men who came to the gym were all brawn with little brains. Maggie helped them no matter what their personality. Women were there for a variety of reasons too, and Maggie treated everyone with kindness, paying attention to each client and their particular needs. She turned with the carafe in her hand to find Maggie sitting at the table, hands folded in front of her, and an angelic smile on her face. Rayne melted inside.

"That's much better. For a minute I thought I was going to have to spank you." As the words left her mouth she wanted to grab them back and stuff them where they'd never be found. Her cheeks heated. Fortunately for her, Maggie's sense of humor kicked in, saving her from further embarrassment.

"Well, that would be something different to try." Maggie raised one brow and rested her chin in her upturned palm.

Rayne's mouth fell open at the implication, making Maggie break into a fit of laughter.

"Relax, Rayne. I was kidding. Mostly." Maggie regained her composure while she stood deathly still. "Are you going to hold that all night or are you actually going to let me have some? I could really use a cup right about now."

The comment got her moving. She smiled and forced her feet forward. Two more steps and she was within pouring range. Once both cups were filled, she gratefully sat. Some hostess she turned out to be. Maggie pulled a Danish from the bag and placed it on the plate in front of her. The cheese bear claw was one of her favorites, causing her mouth to water. When Maggie didn't do the same for herself, Rayne asked, "Aren't you having anything?" There was a twinkle in Maggie's eye indicating she shouldn't have asked.

"I thought it'd be more fun if you fed me." She wriggled her brows up and down a few times before reaching inside the bag again.

She threw her napkin at Maggie. "You're impossible! Can't you see I'm having a hard enough time here?" Rayne was confused and curious about Maggie's reason for the late-night visit, and she hoped whatever was going on, Maggie was okay. Rayne chewed her bottom lip as she fixed her coffee. When she looked up, Maggie was staring at her with a glint in her eye, making it hard to tell if it was mischievous or something else. At least, she hoped it was all kidding on Maggie's part, but who knew? She had her own conflicted reactions, and the recurring dream wasn't helping matters. She didn't even want to think about what Maggie was feeling.

"Why are you having a hard time?" Maggie asked as she reached for the cream.

Rayne froze mid-stir. That was the ultimate question. She stalled for time while she finished fixing her coffee, lifted the mug, and blew across the surface before taking a sip. It was still too hot, but it was strong and good, and gave her a chance to come up with an answer. "I don't know."

"I think I do," Maggie offered.

"Really? Then do share. Inquiring minds want to know." She watched intently as Maggie became quiet. Thoughtful. A plethora of emotions crossed her face as she gazed at her. Maggie had helped

Rayne find her confidence and purpose again. She also helped her realize there wasn't anything she couldn't do, once she decided to move forward instead of staying in the post-Heather haze that had kept her inert for a few months. Maggie had been her cheerleader since the first day.

"I think…" Maggie hesitated for a second as she blew out a big breath. "We both feel *something*, but that doesn't mean we have to act on it."

She didn't want to feel deflated. It had been a boost to her ego to think someone like Maggie found her attractive and maybe, just maybe, a small part of her wanted to enjoy it.

"It's not what you wanted to hear, is it?"

"I'm not sure." Rayne took a breath. She didn't have any right to feel let down. Maggie hadn't done anything to lead Rayne to believe there was more behind the glances that set her heart racing or the all-too-professional touches. When had she started thinking of Maggie in a sexually romantic way? She was just settling into her comfort zone and had even gone to the queer lounge a few times on her own. There was a new level of self-confidence when she embraced the idea she could act in the ways that made her happy. Rather than enjoying those moments, she was hanging on to an erotic dream and the first person who'd shown her any sort of attention, knowing all along her feelings might be one-sided. That was until Maggie had revealed her own thoughts about Rayne.

"We've got a great friendship. I'm hoping we can keep building on that."

The breath she let go of hurt as much as it helped. "Of course. No need to muddy the waters." She set down her mug and broke off a small piece of pastry. The texture would have been nice if her mouth wasn't so dry, and she had to swallow past the lump in her throat.

"That doesn't mean I lied when I said I'd thought about us. I just…" Maggie wrapped her hands around the mug as if to ward off a chill. "The wellness center is really important to me and if I pursue a relationship, you or the dream might suffer. Maybe even both, and that wouldn't be fair to you. Despite my reputation as a player, I do have some ethics and you're someone I never want to hurt because the timing sucked."

It made sense, of course. Rayne could see the struggle written so plainly on her face. Maggie had to choose what was best, and she'd chosen to follow her dream. Like Heather had followed hers. Being on the losing end sucked, but it was better than being strung along for nothing. "I understand."

"I'm not sure you do and I'm probably fucking up something that could be wonderfully perfect."

"Or not." She pointed to the carafe. "Would you like more?"

"Let me," Maggie said before she refilled her near empty cup before filling her own.

Rayne couldn't leave things up in the air, which was how it felt. "So, where do we go from here?"

"We keep doing what we've been doing, unless you don't want to. We see each other at the gym, have dinners together, go to the movies. Have fun." Maggie shrugged. "I'm not here to end the connection we have, Rayne. I'm here to keep it intact."

Relief flooded through her. It wasn't exactly what she'd hoped for, but she wasn't willing to throw it all away because of a romance she'd concocted in her mind. "That's good." She glanced at the steam rising from her cup. "You've been good for my ego." She laughed.

"And here I thought you were only fond of my training skills."

"There's definitely nothing wrong with *your* ego." Rayne shook her head and smiled. Maggie always had a keen sense of humor.

"There is one thing I need to know before I get out of here so you can get more sleep."

Rayne sat back in the chair, dreading what she was about to say. "What is it?" she asked around the food that refused to go down and she reached for her drink.

"Exactly what was I doing in this dream of yours?"

That was the moment the buttery, flaky goodness went down the wrong pipe and she aspirated. Maggie rose, but Rayne waved her off, coughing hard into her napkin for several long seconds before she was able to take another swig. She swallowed without showering the table with the remnants. There was no way she could tell Maggie she'd looked to find her face buried between her spread thighs with her fingers inside. "I...I can't."

Maggie's mischievous grin widened. "That good, huh?" She laughed.

It was better than good, but Maggie might not ever know. The details would remain a secret, and she'd continue to wonder if it would be just as good in person. Would Rayne ever have a meaningful relationship or was destiny determined to steer her away from where her mind constantly wandered?

Rayne woke with the bedding twisted like a cyclone. The sheets were wrapped around her like a protective cocoon. The last thing she remembered about her latest dream was Maggie's knowing smile reflected at her in the gym mirror.

The middle of the night meeting ended after they managed to have a few laughs and a short—very short—discussion that ended with a clear understanding of where Maggie's attention was focused. Perhaps. There remained a glimmer of hope, even with both of them agreeing nothing intimate would happen.

Maggie hadn't pressed for details of the dream, letting Rayne leave the topic behind while being mindful how flustered she was at Maggie having mentioned it. Rayne had her own fears of future relations ending the same way her split with Heather had. Before Maggie left, they agreed on having their usual dinner together at the end of the week, keeping to their routine, and reinforcing the notion that what they had was good. It *was* good, even if the flirting cropped up here and there.

The clock blared neon green numbers. Seven forty. It had been late when Maggie left. When she fell into bed, the clock read one fifty in the morning. She should get out of bed. Today was a workout day. She hadn't missed a planned day since starting Maggie's suggested routine. Not going might make Maggie think it was because Rayne didn't want to be around her, and it would be a lie.

The groaning noise as she rolled out of bed could have been mistaken for pain, though the only pain was her amped up libido and the vision of tiny rivulets of sweat that dripped down Maggie's chest and disappeared into her sports bra. Shuffling along the floor like she was facing penance was a pathetic way of showing her appreciation for Maggie's encouragement throughout her physical achievements. Rayne was invested in continuing to build on those results. With the coffee pot promising to give the life blood she depended on, a shower was next. *Once I've had a shower, I'll feel much better about going.* She pulled her favorite outfit from the dresser and started her bathroom ritual. Some people didn't shower before working out, but Maggie was there, and she'd die of embarrassment if she walked through the door smelling the same way she would when she walked out.

Forty minutes later, she sat nursing a second cup of coffee and dreading the prospect of facing Maggie more and more. With as much resolve as she could muster, she grabbed her bag and car keys before heading out the door, determined to embrace her destiny.

❖

"Hi, Maggie."

Maggie looked up and smiled. Her eyes twinkled the same way they always did. *See, this isn't so bad.*

She gave a little wave and headed for the locker room, glad Maggie was busy with a new customer. Hopefully, she'd be a while and Rayne would have time to settle down, telling herself nothing had changed between them. Rayne stowed her bag, put in her hot pink earbuds, and found a playlist on her phone. After grabbing a towel and a bottle of water from the supply room, she headed out. Today's schedule included a slow run, elliptical, and upper body. *You can do this.* With a nod to herself, she spun around and ran smack into Maggie, the customer she'd been talking with right behind her.

"Oh." Rayne gasped. Heat from her embarrassment traveled through her. Maggie grabbed her shoulders. Luckily for her, Maggie was strong enough to keep them upright. Once she had her feet under her again, Maggie slowly let go.

"Rayne, are you okay?" Her tone was full of concern, but an amused smile turned up the corners of her lips.

The woman behind her stared curiously at the exchange. For a brief instant, Rayne imagined the woman saw there was more of a connection between them than a gym member and an instructor. "Oh, yes. I'm fine. Thanks." She awkwardly smiled at the woman. "I need to go start my routine. Catch you later." She rushed by and headed for the treadmills, wishing Maggie had not just touched her.

Rayne was totally zoned out when she felt a tap on her shoulder. Maggie stood with her arms crossed in front of her. There'd never been a time when Rayne had seen her mad, but she would have bet money she was pretty pissed. She slowed to a cool down pace and pulled one earbud out. "Hi." Her voice was breathy, but at least she wasn't panting, or about to pass out. She glanced away, then back. "Something wrong?" She had a deep drink of water to break eye contact. There were four empty treadmills, so she was pretty sure Maggie's annoyance wasn't about her time on the machine.

"I was going to ask you the same thing. That was a pretty icy greeting for a friend."

Her words resembled an adult chastising a child for rude behavior. To a degree, she was right. Maggie hadn't done anything wrong. Rayne was the one who had the issue. Lacking a better excuse, Rayne looked at her shyly. "I know. I'm sorry. It just feels different…seeing you here…not like when we're outside of your workplace." It was a lame excuse, but Maggie was the one who'd brought up the employee/client issue. She couldn't shake the made-up vison of Maggie naked. With the improbable prospect of seeing Maggie's body, Rayne craved the unknown more and more. That wasn't good for either one of them.

"Since when?" Maggie's eyebrows were knit, and her lips were pursed. "You know, there was a time when I could trust you to be honest. I'm not so sure anymore."

This time Rayne regretted telling Maggie a half-truth and watched Maggie retreat to the far side of the gym. She sat on a bench, then reclined under the barbell and began lifting. Even from where Rayne stood, she could see how the veins bulged on Maggie's neck. *Uh-oh, she's really pissed.* Her inner voice was tssk-tssking. Maggie's friendship was more important than any insecurities about what might happen between them. Ashamed of her behavior, she pulled up her big girl panties and headed in her direction.

CHAPTER TWENTY-ONE

Maggie set the bar back on the rack and sat up. Rayne stood a couple of feet away, her gaze guarded. Wary. As though she was worried if she got too close there'd be a scene. Not likely, but it hurt if that's what she was thinking. Maybe putting on the brakes had affected Rayne more than she let on. "Do you need something, Rayne?" Maggie kept her tone cool and professional. She was hurting, too, and the main reason she wouldn't get involved with anyone was knowing there'd be pain at some point. Sure, the business was important, but in truth she was using it as a convenient excuse to keep distance from her growing attraction.

"I need to apologize, Maggie. I'm more than a little sorry. I've been acting like a jerk."

She counted to ten. The wait felt like hours, although it couldn't have been because a second was a second. When she stood and Rayne flinched, she was close to making her own apology, but she wasn't the one who started this little showdown. If this was anyone else, she'd blast them in her best don't-fuck-with-me tone. But it was *Rayne*, and she couldn't chance losing her for good if that's the card she played. Shit happened. It wasn't like she hadn't ever thought of Rayne in her bed, but the hot and cold on her part needed to end. "Apology accepted. You're right. You have been acting like an ass." She wasn't above making her squirm though.

In a quiet voice, Rayne replied, "I said jerk, not ass." The twitching of her mouth kind of gave her away. It was good to know the teasing was in fun.

"Rayne…" She spoke softly. "Obviously, there's still things we need to hash out." Her resolve from last night melted away, and she was afraid no matter how hard she tried, Rayne would remain in her thoughts. What came next?

"Yes, we do." Rayne agreed, nodding. "The sooner the better. Are you free tonight?"

Heat warmed her cheeks. It happened a lot around Rayne. She didn't often get embarrassed, so why was she feeling so vulnerable? "Uh, not tonight." She paused for a second. "Tomorrow night I teach a class." There was something in Rayne's eyes that made Maggie believe she was hurt by her not being available. Maybe she'd inadvertently triggered something from her past.

"Okay. How about Tuesday?" Rayne asked, her hip cocked.

Maggie studied her phone. "That works. Restaurant or delivery?"

"Let's order in."

She contemplated the options by rubbing her brow. Maggie thought about where they would be more comfortable. "Do you mind if we eat at your place? I'll pick up dinner."

"I'll get something to go with coffee that we won't have to feel too guilty about later."

The smile that made Maggie's heart pound appeared. "That would be nice." She pressed her hands to her thighs as the tension between them built. "Okay then. I'll be at your place around six thirty?"

"Perfect." Rayne turned toward the locker room.

She reached for Rayne and wrapped her fingers around her wrist. "It's going to be okay," she said, reassuringly. "*We're* going to be okay."

Rayne nodded. "I hope so." Rayne squeezed her hand, then walked away.

She sure as hell hoped so too, for both their sakes.

❖

Maggie pushed herself harder. She'd enrolled in a three-hour course with a combination of tai chi and yoga, thinking it would be easy after all the workouts she did on a regular basis. She couldn't have been more mistaken. Her body was in positions she could not have imagined would tax her the way they were. Sweat trickled down the sides of her face. She almost wished she'd begged off for dinner with Rayne rather than continue to punish herself in ways that were physically exhausting, which made her feel less-than. Her original thought was including both types of classes at her business. Now she wasn't so sure.

"Is everyone sufficiently warmed up for yoga?" The instructor, a sixty-five-year-old woman, had been able to make all the tai chi movements look fluid, her breathing deep and unlabored.

The class, some of whom were not unfamiliar with the ancient practice, all appeared relaxed, and everyone was smiling. The instructor called a ten-minute break before they began part two. The supplied bottles of water were at room temp, which was perfect for her to down the entire contents. She pressed a towel to her forehead, over her neck, and down her shoulders. She stretched and pulled and worked her throbbing muscles. As she moved her hand over her forearm, she remembered how Rayne had reached for her during dinner. Maggie wanted her touch though she wasn't pursuing it. No wonder Rayne had expressed her confusion regarding the mixed messages, all because she didn't know how to handle her attraction for Rayne. Maggie had an idea why she'd been standoffish when she came into the gym and that was another reason they needed to talk, though three nights away would feel like an eternity. She was going to have to come up with a way to explain what was going on in her own head, but that would depend on the direction of their conversation. She'd done so well leading the last time, she hoped Rayne would jump in and take charge.

"Okay, everyone, let's get ready. Shoes off and two arm spaces between you and your neighbors. Back, front, and side."

She lined up her shoes with all the others and got a spot toward the front of the room. Maggie hoped she could follow as the instructor slowly demonstrated the named positions. They seemed simple enough, but she was more brawn than grace. All the participants spread their feet a few inches apart, put their palms together, and bowed in greeting. She was ready, but for what she wasn't sure.

CHAPTER TWENTY-TWO

Rolling to her side, Rayne peeked with one eye open at the clock. Two twelve. Ugh. Thoughts of what Maggie's commitment had been plagued her. Not like it was any of her business. For the rest of the evening, she had paced and cursed at herself, being unjustifiably mad Maggie had plans. It hadn't even been twenty-four hours since she'd been flirting and joking with Rayne.

"And you turned the whole conversation into a weird, uncomfortable thing." The inner voice tried to make her look at it from Maggie's point of view. She clearly believed becoming romantically involved would not be good for them. Sometime between then and now, Maggie had decided not to wait for an end to their wishy-washy interactions, the ones that were exciting and confusing and downright irrational. She had every right to do whatever she wanted with whomever she wanted. Like it or not, Rayne had more or less shoved her into the mindset that there was no future involving more than what they had, yet the door continued to feel open.

That reasoning worked right up until she remembered Maggie's reaction when Rayne asked her to dinner yesterday. As if she had gotten caught doing something she didn't want Rayne to know about. Then it hit Rayne. *OMG! She had a date!* Her tossing and turning hadn't been for some random excuse. So, here she was, trying to fight off images of Maggie—a naked Maggie—having hot, passionate sex with another woman. Every time she closed her eyes,

Maggie was there. Her body glistening from misty sweat, like when she worked out. Only this time it was because she was exerting her energy with someone else. She would be even more handsome with the flush of heated passion spreading along her body. Rayne *knew* that's how she'd look. Her lips swollen from crushing kisses.

"That's it! Stop it right now!" Rayne threw back the covers and got out of bed in one motion, then wrestled into her robe as she stomped to the kitchen. Once there, it was a toss-up. Eat something really, really bad or have a cup of tea?

"Staying healthy is all about compromises, Rayne. Make smart choices the majority of the time and you can have whatever you want the rest."

Cripes. Maggie was even in her subconscious. Decision made, she opted for a compromise. A cup of decaf tea and two sugar-free cookies. The whole while the water heated Rayne couldn't stop thinking of anything but the tight, toned body that had been so close to hers for the last six months. She shuffled back to bed with her head hanging in shame. *You sure fucked this up. Way to go, Rayne.*

"Ugh. Already?" Rayne reached for the alarm. She'd gotten to sleep around three, a few short hours ago. Sunday mornings were meant for sleeping in and she had no idea why the alarm was set for a wake-up, especially for seven. She pulled the covers over her head like a teenager who refused to go to school and forced herself back to sleep, determined to stay in bed at least another hour.

The dark sunglasses did nothing to keep the sunlight at bay. The onslaught of stabbing pain continued, and Rayne pulled the car into a parking space as close to the door as she could find. Her head pounded from not enough sleep, and she needed a mega dose of caffeine. Now. She ran for the relative darkness of the supermarket overhang. Retrieving a cart from the rack was another challenge. No matter how much she jiggled, jerked, or growled, it wasn't giving in. She must have looked pathetic as she grumbled under her breath because a stockperson timidly came to her rescue and with one firm yank, unhooked the offending cart from the long line.

"Thanks." Rayne tried for a smile, but it might have been more of a glare, because the young man just nodded and hurried away.

Annoyed didn't begin to describe the feeling that coursed through her, and she stamped her feet in a pathetic tantrum-like fashion, or more like she had to use the restroom in a hurry while waiting for her turn at the Starbucks counter.

The barista's nametag alerted her that Becky would be mixing her elixir and she greeted Rayne with a bright "Good morning! How can I help you?"

She wanted to slap bubbly Becky. Hard. "I need a Venti Pike Place triple espresso with room for cream." Becky must have surmised she was in no mood for banter because she had the cup in her hand before Rayne finished giving her order. In under two minutes the breathless woman placed the steaming cup in front of her and backed away. Rayne raised an eyebrow, wondering how she'd become such an ogre to warrant the reaction. Her nerves settled and she laughed out loud, convinced she was probably losing her mind.

"Is there anything else you need?" Becky's smile had returned.

The urge to ask her if Becky was actually Rebecca from Sunnybrook Farm was on the tip of her tongue. Barely managing to stifle the giggle that threatened to escape, Rayne shook her head. "No, that's all. Thank you, Becky." She used her name and hoped the barista would feel more at ease to take the money she held out. Rayne pulled off her sunglasses and smiled. It must have done the trick because Becky came up to the counter and returned the smile.

"That'll be four eighty-two, please."

She handed Becky a ten-dollar bill and picked up her lifeline to the living. When she attempted to hand back the change, Rayne waved her off.

"Thanks for putting up with me. I had a rough night." She raised the paper cup with the too-thin sleeve and the uncomfortable heat against her fingertips that made her grimace, but she wasn't about to put it down. "Thanks, again." Rayne moved to the self-serve area and added a healthy dose of cream with two Splenda. A quick stir, followed by a long blow across the surface led to the first glorious sip. Pure heaven. As she pressed the lid back on, Becky slid a breakfast bar in her direction.

"Thank you for the tip. I hope your day gets better." Her genuine smile made Rayne realize the day wasn't so bad after all, and she might have made Becky's as well.

"It just did."

❖

"A word of advice: never go to the supermarket hungry without a list."

Rayne's mother shared that sage advice years ago, long before she went to join the Universe as a star, and she could use some advice now. The coffee had helped, but her mind was still foggy, and she wandered aimlessly in the produce section. Every item appeared to be foreign, and she had no clue what to buy. After the fourth or fifth uttered "Excuse me," she yanked her cart out of the way of shoppers who actually knew what they were doing. The smell of fresh baked bread wafted by on air currents caused by people moving about. Rayne's stomach growled. *Did I eat yesterday?* It was hard to remember and harder to think with any clarity before she recalled the bar Becky had given her which she'd carelessly tossed in her bag. Even the wrapper was a challenge, and she was about to give up when it finally gave way. She took a big bite and chewed. The flavor wasn't definable, but it was soft and sweet with bits of nuts, taking the edge off her hunger.

With a couple of swigs left in her cup, she pushed the cart to one of the little bistro tables and found a scrap of paper from her purse. Rayne started a list, knowing she needed staples for the week. Maybe she was just bored with the whole food experience. It was time-consuming and expensive. If it weren't for knowing take-out and prepackaged foods were loaded with salt and unnecessary calories, she wouldn't bother with groceries at all. The only time she got excited about cooking was when she had company. Who was she kidding? The person she looked forward to cooking for the most was Maggie.

Thirty minutes later, her cart was one-third full, and she hummed softly as she shopped. Rayne was delighted when she found a whole section of low-salt, low-fat freshly prepared foods. Some she could freeze for nights she ran late and didn't feel like cooking. Others were guaranteed to stay fresh for five to seven days, giving her time to plan out a menu and cook. She even found a frozen chocolate cream pie that could thaw in the fridge the next time Maggie joined her. That's if she was still interested after their talk.

Living in such an eclectic area was a convenience she wasn't nearly grateful enough for. One block from where she lived there were a number of wonderful little restaurants, shops, coffee houses, and venues for music. Originally, she'd bought her house because it was affordable, and in the five years since then, the neighborhood had blossomed into "the place to be." Her real estate agent, Quinn, had been right. It was an up-and-coming district.

The location was perfect. Rayne liked having a space where she could do what she pleased and doubted she'd ever go back to apartment life.

Aside from loving the house and the area, there was more to consider. Even without knowing what the future held and if it included Maggie.

Her experiments were actually proving at least one of her hypotheses was right and that bit of good news had lifted her spirits. The profession she'd chosen to pursue was hard enough. Most of her income relied on grant funding and if Steve lost funding, she'd have to find another position where she was or move to another institution.

That's likely why she'd latched on to Heather when she brought up the idea of living together. That poor decision had led to the inevitable end. Her ego had been crushed more than her heart, making her wonder if she was capable of being the kind of partner she imagined for herself.

After Heather moved on, she rarely entertained, not that she'd done a lot prior. Heather had crassly mentioned that the house was too old and not something she wanted her "friends" to see. What Rayne saw as charming, Heather saw as not affluent enough for her rising social status. In the end, that's how she'd treated Rayne, too. She should have known then the only reason she stayed was for the sex, but even that wasn't enough. Rayne hadn't been enough. A few months ago, she would have agreed. That wasn't the case anymore. She was intelligent, fun, and ambitious. Rayne had a new appreciation for her curves. She had learned how to love herself, and all she had to do was find the person who appreciated the woman she was, knowing all along she already had.

Chapter Twenty-three

In the checkout line that wasn't moving, Rayne had time to think about her life choices and how to proceed. She should tell Maggie that her nighttime visions were, in part, responsible for her awkward and confusing behavior.

She tossed the pros and cons around, arguing back and forth with herself. In the end, Rayne conceded Maggie needed to know why she'd been acting out of sorts and think about how she wanted to handle Maggie's possible reaction. Maybe her constant worrying was for nothing. Maggie was her friend. It wasn't too late to make amends and show her how much Rayne regretted not being honest with her. It was funny how they always choose to discuss serious issues over food. The body guru and the wannabe. She giggled at the idea. The clerk smiled. He probably wondered what was funny, but she likely wasn't the first person to act strange in his line.

"There's a lot of corresponding data, but the outliers are going to need to be sussed out of the results." Rayne could hardly contain her excitement. She'd been working on this arm of research for over two years. It was an extension of her thesis project, and the results from her latest experiment were proof she'd been on the right track by following her gut. When the body's immune system responded to an invasion of antigens, usually a virus, the body sent out specific cells to combat the infection. But not everyone had the same response and not all immune systems worked the same way. Rayne wanted to know if genetic markers in specific patients dictated a response, or lack thereof, and why some people became extremely ill with a particular infection while others displayed mild symptoms, which in some cases were the majority of the population.

"This could be huge," Steve said as he focused on the bar graph. "Definitely a paper or two. Maybe even a grant." He smiled.

"I don't want to get too excited, but…" Rayne wasn't one to rely on unrealistic expectations. She let out the breath that had been caught in her chest and recognized the feeling of hope, because that's what her life had now. Hope. That hadn't happened since she'd fallen in love with basic science, and then research. "It does look promising."

Science wasn't as much about proving a theory as it was *disproving* a known assumption. It was the unknown that was the science part. Getting there was a journey. Sometimes frustrating and sometimes, like now, exciting. Being overly optimistic about preliminary data would be foolish. Just because this result showed promise didn't mean a repeat of the exact same experiment would give similar results. Those were the pitfalls of science. Though when it worked the way a researcher believed it would and it could be duplicated several times over, then and only then could it be considered a proven theory. It was a longshot and Rayne liked the odds of this one showing positive results. Steve handed the papers back.

"I'm going to do a little documentation in my lab book and work out a duplication schedule."

Steve placed his hand on her shoulder. "There's a future for you here, Rayne. I like having you in my lab and you're a great teacher for the newbies, but in a few years I suspect you'll have a lab of your own if you want one." He looked a little sad. "Enjoy your bench time. You won't get as much once the world knows your name."

"Uh, thanks, Professor." She hadn't even considered what advancement in her career would mean to the work she loved carrying out under his wing. The best instruments, helpful and supportive faculty, and a great opportunity to someday be on a tenure track. Steve spoke about not being on the bench, and she hadn't given any thought to how little she saw him working in the lab. He wasn't MIA all the time. There were lab meetings and other events where everyone got together to discuss the latest paper or talk about a seminar speaker that they should invite.

Rayne couldn't imagine giving up her experiments and not seeing the results of her labor. The duplication of cells in a petri dish. The lack of infection in her colony that was due to treatment with an infusion of a known antibiotic or a cocktail of several. Those moments excited her.

Another thing that excited her was the prospect of spending time with Maggie. How could she leave? Besides, she didn't *want* to leave. They got along so well, only this time there was the possibility of things going awry, and just like her research, she had to be patient and wait for the results.

Rayne rubbed her eyes. Twelve-hour workdays weren't top on her list, but she was proud of all she'd accomplished. The rough draft of a grant proposal based on her latest findings would need more refinement, but it was a good start. Steve had told her to stay home tomorrow and work on her paper. It was one of the perks of having a flexible schedule. Follow-up experiments were plotted out in her lab notebook, and she was excited to see the results. That would have to wait until she had everything she needed. The supplies would arrive over the next few days, giving her time to check and double check her methods and the sequence of events. Science was a lot like a domino game. The result of an experiment would lead to the next step and so on. If the experiment failed and gave unexpected results, the whole plan would have to be reworked.

"Oh well, that's why it's called research." Rayne chuckled and saved the files on her computer before gathering her things to leave. Her phone vibrated in her hand, alerting her she had a missed message. She'd turned it off a few hours ago and her heart did that pitter-patter when she thought it might be Maggie. Instead of feeling elation when she heard the voice, her gut sank.

"Hi, Rayne, it's Heather." Her voice purred into the phone and sent a cold chill down Rayne's spine. "You probably don't want to talk to me." *You think?* "Here's the thing, uh…I forgot my perfume." She paused before rushing on. "Would you be a doll and drop it by the office? Thanks, bye."

Rayne punched the erase key and viciously threw the phone into the depths of her bag before heading for the elevator. Once in her car, she took a few breaths. With the passage of time, she'd hoped the sting of Heather's departure would evaporate, and it had. But the anger that took its place was new for her. There were a lot of new emotions and feelings she'd grown into over the last six months. What was Heather doing back in town? Had her punishment been cut short, or had she connived her way into the good graces of the powers that be, like she always had? All Rayne could to do was shake her head as she parked in the driveway, longing for the sanctity of her home.

There might have been a time when she would have done anything to appease Heather, but now that she had been cut loose, Rayne was determined to do better for herself. She grabbed an unsweetened iced tea, sipping the semi-tart beverage as she turned her attention inward. Once and for all she wanted to rid herself of any remaining feelings for Heather, whether they were good or bad. No matter what she did, the resolve to ignore the message wouldn't go away.

The nerve! She cheats, calls me fat, then wants her stupid perfume! Ugh! She was still trying to manipulate Rayne into being her servant. Ha. Just as she was about to continue her internal tirade, an evil plan formed. She pictured herself, knowing she must look like the Cheshire cat. Heather would get her "perfume."

❖

Revenge. Her inner dyke smiled. She pulled an old plastic bowl from the cabinet and placed it on the back of the toilet. Next, she went to the toolbox in the closet and selected several items. On the way through the bedroom, she grabbed Heather's precious bottle of perfume, some exclusive concoction made by Creed, and took it to the bathroom sink. She was careful not to mangle the soft metal while prying the cap from the glass. It was much easier than she thought it would be. Pouring the stinky liquid down the sink made her smile. She left a little in the tubing of the mister, happy the bottle was tinted. It would be impossible to tell the color was off. Satisfied with her handiwork so far, she headed back to the kitchen for another drink. If she was going to do this, she was all in.

The building where Heather worked loomed large and ominous. Last night's bravado wavered in the light of day. Closing her eyes, Rayne took several deep breaths, willing the confidence to return, wanting to wear it like a badge of honor. This morning, she filled the perfume bottle and replaced the cap with slow precision. If she hadn't known better, she would never have guessed the contents had been removed. The metal gleamed in pristine condition without any sign of having been tampered with.

When she got out of the car, her nerve returned. She was once again pissed for having been shit on. It was one thing to be told she was fat. It was quite another to be told she wasn't good enough. She'd show her good enough. Once inside the building, she asked the powers that be to grant her one final view of Heather getting what she deserved. The elevator slowly dropped from the eighth floor and gave her a chance to put on an impassive mask. Rayne didn't want her to see how angry she was, or she might suspect something. Neither did she want her to think she was crushed by what she'd done. Yes, Rayne had been hurt and humiliated by Heather's words. However, this would prove to be her finest hour. Maybe it was a bit over-the-top. She didn't care. Even if she only managed to see Heather humble for a minute because she wanted something bad enough to pretend things were okay between them.

The former Rayne would have never gone through with an act of vengeance no matter how harmless. Heather's words had stung, but they were true. Rayne deserved better. No matter how unhappy Heather had been, she should have told Rayne. She'd belittled her to make herself feel better. Maybe this wouldn't make Rayne feel better either, but vindication through what Heather earmarked as important was a bit of comfort.

The receptionist eyed her with open admiration, surprising her. Rayne wore her hair spiked and edgy, her makeup evidence of careful application. The royal blue dress clung in all the right places and flowed over the parts of her body that Heather always avoided. The special touches were a spectacular pair of white Jimmy Choos and an aquamarine clutch. The results she saw in the mirror that morning were impressive. She'd smiled at the confident woman in the reflection. All she had to do was keep cool. As she approached the desk, Rayne made sure the fake smile and all the charm she could muster, was in place.

"Good morning. I need to see Heather Lockley." Her voice was confident and strong. None of her anxiety over seeing Heather again showed, though on the inside she was a mess. She remembered to breathe as the woman took her time responding.

"Certainly. I'll let her know you're here, Ms…?"

Duh. Loathing her own stupidity, she answered. "Yes, of course. Rayne Thomas."

The woman blushed and cleared her throat, leading her to believe the woman had heard a great deal about her. Most likely anything but flattery. Rayne grew madder by the second. Her hand tightened on the clutch.

"Is there a problem, Ms…?" she asked curtly. Two could play this game.

The woman recovered with a pleasant smile, and Rayne gave her credit for at least having the decency to cover her shock. "I apologize. I'm Nicole. If you'll have a seat in the waiting area, I'll call Ms. Lockley immediately." Nicole's face paled.

"Thank you." Rayne turned and took a seat in the plush lounge.

Once she was seated and out of earshot, Nicole picked up the phone. Hopefully, she was calling Heather. A thought briefly flashed, and she worried Nicole might be calling Security. Lord knows what Heather had told her coworkers. Nothing Heather did would surprise her now. Maybe there was a time when she wouldn't have thought so. Unfortunately, that time had come and gone.

Five minutes later, the doors behind Nicole opened and she could hear Heather's overly exuberant laughter precede her grand entrance into the lobby. It meant she was nervous. Rayne smiled. She should be.

Rayne stood and met Heather halfway, leaving no room for her to mistakenly presume she had control over the encounter. Before she could say anything and put on a show for Nicole and the little tart following in her wake, she opened her purse and pulled out the Ziploc bag containing her precious bottle. She held it out.

"I believe you wanted this." She waited while Heather looked her over from head to toe and back up again. She hung on to the idea that Heather regretted throwing her away without so much as a second thought.

Unable to hide her surprise, Heather gingerly took the bag. "Uh, thanks. You could have called for me to pick it up."

She wasn't sure where the words came from, but Rayne's comeback was priceless. "What? And miss the opportunity to show your co-workers what you threw away for a fuck and a fast track to the top of the food chain?" If Rayne thought Heather looked shocked before, she was blown clear away by her little diatribe. "Enjoy your perfume. Whoever you're fucking now, I hope they were worth it." She wished she had a camera. Rayne got in the elevator and turned, unable to help smiling as Heather stood with her mouth agape. Heather's assistant, or whoever the hell she was, tapped her on the shoulder, clearly wanting to placate her as she stood there looking like she might have a tiny smidge of regret. The last thing Rayne heard her say made her laugh out loud.

"Damn. She never looked that good with me."

CHAPTER TWENTY-FOUR

Maggie cupped her crotch and crossed her legs as she danced on her feet. She hadn't used the restroom at the restaurant and sitting in the car for the last fifteen minutes as she attempted to formulate the words she wanted to say hadn't helped. Maybe her predicament would start the evening on a funny note, unless she didn't make it to Rayne's bathroom. Then she'd just be embarrassed. She rang the bell and tried not to move. *Please hurry, please hurry, please hurry.*

The door swung open. "Hi. What delectables did you bring me?"

Maggie rushed by Rayne, dropped the bags, and ran down the short hallway.

"Nice to see you, too." Rayne called after her.

She had her jeans undone by the time she got there, barely closing the door before she dropped onto the toilet. Painful relief washed over her as the discomfort left. *That was close.* She felt like a child who refused to stop what they were doing to go to the bathroom. She checked her underwear. Thankfully they were dry. She washed her hands before having to apologize to Rayne, again.

"Hi."

"Feel better?" Rayne smiled as she leaned against the counter.

"Oh my God, yes. That was a close one." Maggie laughed. Now that the crisis was averted she had to admit it was funny.

"I don't want to know how long you waited to go."

"Good." She went to the bags Rayne had moved to the breakfast bar. "Can you turn the oven on? There's a few dishes that need a reheat." She wasn't fond of aluminum containers because it took away using the microwave. She wasn't about to dirty more dishes. That kind of defeated the convenience of takeout. "I thought we'd have food from New World Bistro. Have you been there?"

"Not yet." Rayne smiled again and the warmth of her gaze enveloped Maggie. The tension in her shoulders eased. "Have you eaten there often?" Rayne asked.

"Once or twice for special occasions."

"Is this a special occasion?" Rayne's cheeks became rosy.

Maggie's pulse pounded. Of course, she wanted tonight to be special. "Do *you* want it to be?" The question wasn't intended to be playful, but that's how it came out and now it was too late to fix it.

Rayne's shoulders visibly tensed and her expression was hard to read. Her eyes sparkled, but Maggie didn't think it was in a good way. "Why can't you give me a straight answer?"

What could she say? One part of her was dead set on keeping on course with only casual sexual liaisons. The kind she could keep at arm's length without expectations or a commitment. The other part with the voice that was getting louder every day, wanted more with Rayne because she was the first person since Eve's death that Maggie thought about in a meaningful way. If only she had the courage to say what she was thinking. She needed to tell Rayne about her fear of loss that was even greater than her fear of never opening her business. So, what the fuck was she doing? "I'm sorry." She reached across the space between them, but Rayne moved away.

"Seriously, Mags. This flirting then retreating behavior has to stop."

Maggie inhaled slowly and gathered her tattered wits. "You're right."

"Finally. Was it so hard admitting you're making us both crazy?"

"Did I say that?"

Rayne smiled mischievously. "You didn't have to."

"Would it be okay for tonight to be a date?" She surprised herself for saying what she'd been thinking. She could do this.

"I'm not sure." Rayne nibbled at her bottom lip until she met Maggie's gaze. "But I'm not about to turn down a special dinner. So yes, it's a date."

"Good." Despite her best effort, Maggie's pulse began to race. "Ready for dinner?"

Rayne reached for one of the bottles of wine. "Sure. Do you want wine?"

"Absolutely!" Her enthusiastic reply was a bit much, but Rayne didn't appear to notice. Her mind played out different scenarios as they worked in the small space. At one point their hips brushed and she froze for a second before Rayne laced their fingers and she squeezed. The casual touch had implications of how much they connected, even after the awkward start. A tingle spread through her that she wasn't prepared for, bringing her up short.

"You okay?" Rayne asked as her fingers slipped away.

She grinned like she wasn't embarrassed at all. "I'm fine."

"I've heard the food from this place is very good."

The heat from Rayne's body caressed her skin. Maggie could have become lost in the sensation if she had let the moment take over. It would have been easy enough to do. "I hope you like it." She'd been a wreck picking out items.

Rayne handed her a glass after she slid items into the oven.

"What's on the menu tonight?"

"Bruschetta and charred brussels sprouts to start." She sipped, then set little containers of seasonings and sauces on the table.

"Nice." Rayne was quiet. Not like she had been a hundred times before, bubbling with enthusiasm and talking about a lab result or an interesting paper she'd read.

"What's wrong?"

"Nothing."

She snorted. "We both know 'nothing' means something."

"I like this look on you." Rayne pointed to her clothing.

"Oh." She smiled nervously. "One of the advantages of eating at home." Maggie liked dressing up for their dinner and movie nights, but she spent so much time in gym clothes wearing jeans was a nice change. While they waited Maggie had a decision to make. Forge ahead and confess everything or continue the wishy-washy way she'd been acting for the past few months. Her behavior was unsavory, and she couldn't seem to stop fucking up. "I'm sorry I've been acting like such a jerk."

Rayne lightly touched her hand. "I wouldn't say a jerk, but there's definitely things you aren't saying and that's worrisome."

Maggie's eyes burned. If there'd been a chance, no matter how remote or impossible or unsure, she was certain the spark between them was dying a slow death. She was the one who was dousing the flame. No wonder she was single. Still, she didn't want Rayne to think the worst of her. "I know." The timer beeped, making her jump.

"Let's move to the table." Rayne pulled the appetizers out of the oven and put the remaining containers in.

Maggie brought their glasses and the open bottle to the table. Rayne joined her and touched her arm.

Thank you for bringing dinner."

"You're welcome." She swallowed around the knot. "Tonight is special."

Rayne rubbed her thumb over her knuckles. "I want *us* to be special, Mags."

The shiver was involuntary and very real. Everything happening tonight was real, but what kind of a future did they have if she wasn't willing to get over *her* insecurities? How was she able to help others when she couldn't move forward in her own life? Not being the best version of herself cheated them both from a bright, happy whatever.

"My last relationship was in college." Maggie glanced at the food and picked up her glass. "The one and only relationship I've had, and it ended tragically."

Rayne blanched. "Okay." Rayne sat back, gently breaking the tentative connection.

She shouldn't have started the conversation like she had, but there was no going back. Maggie took a breath. "Eve was…" Damn. Talking about Eve was proving harder than she thought. Then she remembered how much in love she'd been and the grip around her heart loosened. "She was my person." Maggie shook her head at her inability to make her thoughts clear. "I loved Eve so much, and she loved me." Flashes of her beautiful smile and the way she laughed made her realize even though she was physically gone, Eve was still with her.

"First love is amazing." Rayne appeared to understand. When the silence between them stretched out, Rayne asked, "What happened?"

"Eve was full of life. She was involved in important causes. And she loved to run. She was in great shape." She needed to do something with her hands and put food on Rayne's plate before taking a small helping for herself. "She had a massive heart attack and died."

Rayne's hand flew to her mouth. "Oh my God. I'm so sorry." She ran her hand through her unruly hair. The gesture was one Rayne used when she was trying to keep her emotions under control.

"One minute she was vibrant and alive, and the next…" The depth of her grief would likely never go away, but the stabbing pain that had formerly immobilized her was only a dull throb. The progress felt good.

"When did she die?" Rayne played with her food.

"Eight years ago." Some days it felt like yesterday, but they were getting fewer.

"That's a long time, Mags."

"I know." She abandoned eating and refilled their glasses until the bottle was empty.

"You haven't been in a relationship since?"

It was an honest question and one she'd asked herself time and again. "No."

"What about the women from the gym?"

"You mean the casual hook-ups I've had because I'm human and have needs?" Her words had an edge because the question felt like judgement even if Rayne hadn't meant it that way.

"I'm trying to understand where you're coming from and where your head is."

The tension from earlier had slowly disappeared and she didn't want it to interfere with her wanting Rayne to understand why she'd been less than enthusiastic about getting involved. "They were for sex and nothing more." The stove buzzed at the perfect time. "I'll get that."

Rayne took the appetizers to the kitchen. "More wine?" Her voice had that teasing quality that put Maggie at ease.

"Yes." She brought the items to the table and joined Rayne. After they fixed their plates, she glanced up to find Rayne focused on her.

"Does the idea of dating me scare you?"

Maggie admitted tonight *did* feel like a date. "Yes, but probably not for the reasons you think." She'd sabotaged a lot of promising connections before. This time, she was determined to make the most of the opportunity, no matter how it turned out. "How do you feel about dating me?"

"It's felt like we've been dating for a while, but I haven't let myself go there."

"Why not?"

Rayne swallowed her food and slowly took a drink. "Because you run hot and cold. I like the flirty stuff, but that's how the relationship with Heather started, and I'm not going to let myself be blindsided again."

Good friends, solid friends, worked out their differences. If they couldn't get past a few bumps along the way, then it wasn't much of a friendship. Nor would any relationship they might try survive. That's not what she wanted, and she hoped Rayne wouldn't settle for less, no matter who it was. She was too perfect to be treated like a temporary fix. Rayne wasn't a one-nighter. She cared about her too much to play games and she realized that's what she'd been doing up until now.

"I'm not the same woman I once was. Since meeting you, I'm no longer content with superficial relationships. You came to the gym because you wanted more in your life. All you needed was a little confidence boost. You already had the motivation." Maggie took a moment to find the words. "I want the same things. I want a better version of me."

Rayne's face showed she'd turned inward and Maggie wasn't convinced it was a good sign. "When we started doing things outside of the gym, I dove in and embraced your friendship. I don't regret that." Rayne's lips pursed. "Leading me on, then saying you didn't want a relationship hurt. I let my guard down. I was open and vulnerable with you, and you dashed my hopes."

Maggie's heart ached. "I know. What can I do to fix it?"

Rayne shook her head. "It's not something that can be fixed, Mags."

Maggie's heart bottomed out. "I fucked up."

When Rayne laughed her insides settled a little. "Yes, you did." The statement hung in the air. "Let's clean up and move to the living room."

The food that was mostly untouched got stowed in the refrigerator and the dishes were put in the dishwasher. All that was left was the all-important question of whether Rayne was willing to give her another chance.

CHAPTER TWENTY-FIVE

Rayne made up her mind about what to say after puttering in the kitchen for far longer than necessary. Despite how Maggie had behaved recently, Rayne was ready to move their relationship forward. There might not be any assurance that the future would be what she hoped for, but ignoring the truth, her truth, was no longer an option.

Maggie sat in the side chair and looked as determined as Rayne felt. She sat on the couch and patted the cushion next to her.

"Do I need to be ready to run? Because if I do, I'd just as soon stay here." Maggie snickered.

"Very funny. Get your ass over here." After a second, she added, "Please?" If they were going to have a serious heart-to-heart she at least wanted to be close enough to touch her. The space was an arm-length away, but she was glad when Maggie moved beside her. She had insecurities like everyone else and disliked what felt like a deep valley separating them. "I want to know what changed for you."

"Despite the rumors, there's not one person I've been with physically that I want to see again."

Rayne nodded but remained quiet. She hugged a pillow and squeezed. It wasn't a surprise to hear Maggie had been with others, but it made her uncomfortable considering they were talking about relationships. "Why not?"

"The women were so phony; I didn't even consider a relationship. No one could compare to Eve, and I'd resigned myself to being okay with having emotionally unattached sex." Maggie made a point of making eye contact. "That was all before meeting you." Maggie leaned forward and looked down at her hands clasped between her thighs.

"What changed?"

"The more I got to know you, the more I discovered what I wanted in my life. All the qualities that had been missing in those women, I saw in you."

"You never said anything until I brought up the subject. Why not?" Rayne knew she was drilling Maggie, but she had to know.

"I was afraid that getting involved would result in giving up the dream of having my own business. I'd given up a dream before."

"When?" This was all news to her, and she wanted to be sure she understood the whole picture, not just bits and pieces. Maggie drank wine, clearly taking her time before responding. That could be good or bad.

"I studied sports medicine mostly because of the nagging injuries Eve suffered while doing what she loved. When she died, I couldn't bear to keep going and quit for a year. Then a friend suggested I check out medical massage. I loved anatomy and learning about the human body. The two lines of study were similar, and I could apply my first two years of courses to my degree."

Rayne took in all Maggie was saying, reasoning in her mind the parallels between the past and present. "And now you're afraid you'll have to abandon another dream if something happens to our relationship?"

"I know, it sounds crazy, but that's what I believed. Things change. History doesn't have to repeat itself. You aren't Eve and I'm not that emotionally stagnant person who isn't willing to risk her heart to find happiness." Maggie let out a breath and sat back. "But I'm not the only one who didn't let on her true feelings. What made you hold back from saying you wanted more between us?"

Unshed tears blurred her vision. She could do this. "I got scared."

"Scared of what?" Maggie took her hand. The connection felt right.

"I was afraid how much I wanted to be with you…like in my dream." She somehow managed to keep her tears at bay though her cheeks warmed. She straightened her shoulders, steeling herself to keep going. "But not just the sex part. All the other things that make up a relationship that I never cared about with Heather."

"Rayne, I hate to break this to you, but wanting to have sex with another woman is okay." Maggie's eyes were kind, and the corners of her mouth twitched.

"Grr…you ass!" She hit her with the pillow. "I know it's *okay*. I just didn't think it was okay with you." Rayne ran a hand through her hair, then laughed. "We suck at this sharing feelings thing." She finished her wine.

"Let me get more." Maggie's hand moved to her leg.

"Okay." Rayne didn't think she'd be too steady on her feet and was grateful for the offer.

Maggie looked over her shoulder. "I'll be right back."

The night was turning out better than she'd hoped, and she prayed it would continue on a positive note, even though the possibility remained it could all come crashing down. Some things were worth the risk. She was betting on their coming to a mutual understanding.

❖

The air between them crackled with energy. Rayne had followed her to the kitchen.

"On second thought, why don't we have coffee and dessert?"

Maggie let out a breath of relief. She'd started to feel the wine and crashing on Rayne's sofa would test her resolve. If the day came for intimacy, she didn't want it to be alcohol fueled. She'd done enough of that over the last few years.

"That sounds good." She stood next to the breakfast bar, her hands shoved deep in her pockets. "How can I help?"

"There's a bakery box in the refrigerator that can go on the table."

Glad for a task to keep her nerves at bay, Maggie did as instructed. Rayne handed her plates, napkins, and forks.

"I hope you don't mind dark roast. I've found the most amazing coffee and want your opinion."

Maggie chuckled. "I'm a wine snob for sure, but I'll give the coffee a go." While the coffee brewed, she excused herself. Once behind the closed bathroom door, she stared at her reflection. "You can do this. Being with Rayne is all you've thought about and it's time to act. Not all relationships end in tragedy. Don't be a coward." Time to do what she came there to do and find out if Rayne was willing to move forward. She was hopeful the answer would be yes, but there was a thread of worry it might already be too late.

Rayne sat at the table pouring coffee.

"Is that from Wells Farm?" They had a signature stamp on all their pie crusts, but it was hard to tell with the sugar on top.

"It is. You've raved about them so much, I decided to see if I share your opinion." Rayne cut into it and produced a perfect slice of raspberry pie. "There were so many fruit pies, I had a hard time deciding."

"Raspberry is my favorite." She could hardly wait to dig in.

"I know."

Maggie couldn't remember talking about pies, but then there'd been a number of times when she was so enamored by Rayne she zoned out. She needed to pay more attention.

"What are you waiting for? Dig in." Rayne forked a piece off and slid the fork into her mouth. The way she wrapped her lips around it and pulled it out clean was sexy as hell. As she chewed, her eyes closed. "Mmm, it's so good."

"Yes, it is." Maggie could watch Rayne for hours and not grow tired of the view.

Rayne tipped her head. "You haven't tasted it."

She gave herself a mental shake. "Uh, I've had it before." They ate in relative silence, savoring each forkful. When they were finished, she held her mug between her hands. "Have you decided if dating is something you're willing to try?" Her stomach tightened.

"Of course, I have." Rayne sipped from her mug and looked at her through her thick lashes. Time stood still. "Do you mean dating you?"

Maggie knew her mouth was open, but nothing came out.

Rayne laughed. "Sorry, that was cruel." She reached across the table and slid her fingers beneath hers. "Yes. I'd like to date you."

The whoosh of air that escaped was audible. "You had me worried for a minute." This was good. "Okay. Good. We're dating." The butterflies that batted around in her stomach were ones of excitement instead of dread. Now all she had to do was prove she was in it for the long haul.

CHAPTER TWENTY-SIX

It had only been a couple of days since they'd met for coffee, but the thought of having to wait until the weekend had Maggie doing double time at the gym. She called Rayne asking if she had time for a pizza, using the excuse of dropping off revised pages for the grant application, but that wasn't the real reason she had to see Rayne. They stood in the living room under the pretense of saying good night.

Maggie looked at Rayne's full, red-tinged lips. She wanted to kiss them. She needed to know how they felt beneath her own. Believing if she asked permission she'd be denied, Maggie slowly moved closer. She heard Rayne pull in a quick breath when she realized what was about to happen and Maggie paused for the briefest moment before she leaned in. Rayne's lips were warm and soft. When her lips parted and she slipped her tongue inside, Maggie closed her eyes and moaned. She would have deepened the kiss if it were not a defining moment for both of them. If she went too far, would Rayne withdraw?

If she was counting, tonight was their third official date. If she did not finish the kiss, she would regret the missed opportunity. She slipped out and traced Rayne's lips with the tip of her tongue. Maggie trembled when Rayne pulled away. They stood staring into each other's eyes, sharing a perfect, intimate moment.

Rayne placed her hand lightly against the space below Maggie's throat and wistfully smiled. "Maggie, I..."

Maggie pressed her fingertips gently to Rayne's mouth. "Don't. Please. One kiss…that's all I wanted." She brushed Rayne's bangs from her eye. "Okay?" Maggie cupped the side of Rayne's face and her eyes fluttered in response.

"Okay." Rayne covered Maggie's hand with her own. "I'm not going to lie to you. I *have* thought about what kissing you would feel like for a while. Before the dream stirred things to a dangerous point."

"Fantasizing over me might not be healthy for our relationship. I'd hate to disappoint you by being an underachiever." Even as she said the words, a shiver ran through Maggie, and she pushed away the desire thrumming through her body. When would it be appropriate to have sex with Rayne? Funny, she'd never thought about that when she slept with anyone before, but this was different. Maggie didn't think of her in terms of no strings attached sex. Rayne was her girlfriend and she needed to be respectful of Rayne's boundaries, whatever they were. But her attraction to Rayne was not to be ignored forever. She liked curvy women. Since the first time she saw her, she thought Rayne was sexy, and vividly remembered the day they spoke. She thought back to that day again, reliving the moment.

Rayne's thumb brushed against her cheek, bringing her back to the here and now. "What do you mean, Mags?"

Maggie shook her head to clear it. "Sex is important in a romantic relationship, and I don't want to disappoint you." She tentatively placed her hands on Rayne's hips. "I have to go." Desire coursed through her limbs and settled low in her belly. If she were to give in to her libido, she would be pleading her case and begging Rayne to let her stay. She hugged Rayne to her and whispered in her ear. "You are so beautiful. You've always been beautiful. I don't want you to regret having sex when it happens, and I don't want you second-guessing my motives for coming here tonight. That's the only reason I'm not asking to stay, because believe me when I tell you this—I want to fulfill your fantasies, and mine." She let go, smiling and knowing there'd be a right time. She softly kissed Rayne's forehead. "Good night, babe."

She left Rayne standing in the middle of the living room. Once outside, she took in big gulps of fresh air. In the car, she watched Rayne's house for a minute, torn between hoping against hope she'd open the door and call her back. But part of her was grateful. Rayne was worth the wait and Maggie was encouraged she'd been able to stop herself from doing what she'd always done by ending a date with a fuck. That meant something. Right?

When there was no sign of Rayne, Maggie started her car and drove away. She'd send a text before bed and tomorrow she would call and check on her. A lot had happened in a short amount of time. It was good to know her approach was more rational and less impulsive. Though if they waited much longer before having sex, she was certain her clit would explode.

The department office was exceptionally quiet when Rayne stopped at the administrator's desk. "Hi, Deb. Any messages?"

Deb smiled back at her, revealing her white teeth and sparkling eyes. "Just a few. They're in your email." She grabbed one of the many folders neatly stacked over the surface of her desk and pulled out a few pages. "Nothing urgent in them, but these came late Friday."

The signature pages for the cost center established on the new grant Steve had received gave her the ability to authorize orders in his absence, since she was his backup. Rayne began to sign where the little Post-it arrows stuck out from the edge of each page. She glanced around as she worked. "Where is everyone?"

Deb looked out the office door before lowering her voice. "Bigwigs are coming for a meeting tomorrow, so everyone's catching up on backlogs." She rolled her eyes. Deb knew just about everything that went on in the office, including the way a lot of the employees neglected their work until a deadline loomed. She constantly helped to put out fires and Rayne wondered why she put up with it. "Something you don't have to worry about." She laughed. "You're one of the few who understands what's urgent and what's not."

She appreciated the comment. "If you need help dealing with all the last-minute demands, please let me know." It had been more than a few years since she'd graduated from a snot-nosed graduate student to a postdoc. Back then, she hadn't truly appreciated how much Deb did for students, let alone everyone else, and keeping people on track so these types of visits went smoothly was among the many things she did that weren't part of her job description.

"Thanks, Rayne. I'll manage." Deb took the papers and looked them over.

She tapped her fingers on the counter to get Deb's attention and added, "You always do."

Rayne quietly closed the door behind her and embraced the sanctuary of her office. It was a place she'd come to love over the last year. When Rayne was still with Heather, it was the one place Heather couldn't try to control. Looking back, it was also one of the few places Heather wasn't able to wield her sex appeal to get what she wanted. Rayne silently gloated about being able to keep her out due to the security measures in place. Of course, if she'd wanted, Rayne could have gotten her in as a visitor, but Heather had the ability to command whatever space she was in, and Rayne enjoyed being on a level playing field with her place in the team. The men in research were all happily married as far as Rayne knew, and she had no intention of exposing them to someone who often came across as "over-the-top."

Well, she's out of my life and I have no one to answer to. She remembered the look on her face the day she'd delivered the perfume. The thought was freeing as much as it made her sad. There might still be hope for Maggie, but she had no intention of kidding herself. She'd been clueless once, and the last thing she wanted was to fuck up another relationship because she was too wrapped up in her work. While it was true she loved what she did and had always held on to the belief she could have it all by sharing her life with someone, maybe it was a future that wasn't meant for her.

Rayne fixed a cup of coffee from her personal Keurig and brought it to her desk. After signing in, she checked her email for the messages Deb had sent and saw that there were two. The first was from her doctor's office reminding her of an upcoming appointment. She checked both her work calendar and her phone, making sure she wouldn't miss it. The second was from Steve, asking if they could go over the manuscript she had started earlier in the week. She typed a quick response and was about to keep going to clear out the junk in her inbox when her phone dinged with an incoming message.

She often ignored interruptions, but she hadn't started anything that needed her undivided attention, and she flipped her phone over to look at the screen. Maggie's name appeared. Her wallpaper was a picture of them standing on an outcropping with a mountain range in the background, and they were both smiling. Rayne saw what she'd been missing. A sparkle in their eyes. Her arm was around Maggie's waist and Maggie was hugging her close. They looked happy.

Her heart pounded fast and hard. She had spent a long time last night lying in bed thinking about the kiss. It had been poignant and heated. It had also ended way too soon. While she readied for work, Rayne tried to keep the excitement of that moment at bay. Maggie had assured her she wanted more, but in the back of Rayne's mind, the doubt wasn't easily dismissed. She clicked on the message icon and held her breath as she read.

Hi. I hope you are having a great morning. Last night was... perfect. The only thing I wish was for the kiss to have never ended. Maybe I'll see you at the gym later? - Mags.

The sensation of that kiss lingered on her lips. Maggie's mouth was soft and gentle, but Rayne was sure beneath it lay a smoldering fire of passionate heat with hard edges and a sharp tongue. She'd wanted to explore her mouth but held back, and the idea of going after what she wanted thwarted the desire, and turned it into inaction. She wasn't the only one. It was clear from Maggie's message she had wanted more too, and she questioned why she'd stopped and left. Only one way to find out. Rayne pressed reply.

Why did you stop? Send.

She left the phone face up and continued to read through her emails, tagging a few and trashing others. Every few seconds, she glanced over at the screen, wanting to be sure she didn't miss Maggie's message. Rayne needed the distraction. *May as well get some work done.* It could be hours before Maggie saw the message. Her clientele could be so demanding. She smiled at her own joke.

A little while later, the phone rang, startling her out of her preoccupation with daydreams. "Good morning. This is Rayne." She typed a response to an inquiry in an email. There were times when she had dozens of pieces of correspondence to answer. Today was one of those days. It was tiring and time-consuming. One of her least favorite parts of her job. She'd rather be at the bench or writing up a draft paper. Besides, what ever happened to picking up a phone and hashing stuff out without technology as the middleman? She shook her head.

"There's a Ms. Flanders asking to see you," Deb said, her voice breathy.

Rayne stared at the phone in disbelief. This had to be her imagination at work. She could have sworn she said Flanders. "I'm sorry. Could you repeat that please?"

"Ms. Flanders is here."

Oh my God. She jumped up. Maggie had never come to her workplace. Thinking something must be wrong, she tried to calm down. "Please show her the way, Deb. I'll meet her in the hall." Her voice was high-pitched and strained. By the time she got out the door, Maggie was taking long, slow strides toward her. She stopped a few feet away.

"Hi." Maggie's voice was low and husky. Her eyes held Rayne's steadily. "I'm sorry to interrupt you at work. I can go if this is a bad time."

"No." She leaned against the wall hoping it wasn't obvious she needed something to hold her up. "Aren't you working?" What day was it? All rational thought had left the building.

"I'm covering for Jill at two o'clock."

"Is something wrong?"

Maggie's smile was infectious, and Rayne smiled back. "Nothing's wrong. I wanted to come and answer your question, in person." She moved nearer, closing the distance between them.

Rayne's pulse raced, her blood rushing through her veins. "What?" Thrown by Maggie's appearance, she was lost. Her thoughts were a jumble of scattered fragments. Maggie's crystal blue eyes sparkled with life. If she focused hard enough, could she see her very soul and know her intentions? Maggie took another step. Only a foot separated them.

Maggie's mouth quirked. "I stopped because I didn't want you to think a kiss was all I wanted." Maggie took the last step that separated them. Her mouth was mere inches away. "Is this your office?"

Rayne watched as she slowly licked her lips, making it nearly impossible to concentrate on what she was saying. "Uh-huh."

"Can we go inside?"

Why was the ability to think so difficult? She glanced over her shoulder to be sure it really was her office before she stepped inside. It wasn't a big office. A few more steps and she was against her desk with nowhere to go as Maggie shut the door. *Focus.* What had Maggie said? Not the kiss. "If not for a kiss, why did you kiss me?" Rayne kept flicking her gaze between Maggie's eyes and her mouth. She wanted to feel those lips again. Everywhere. Maggie leaned in, placing her hands next to hers on the edge of the desk. Her heart pounded in her ears. Maggie's lips parted and Rayne was convinced she was going to kiss her. Instead she tipped her head and gently sucked the pounding pulse point of her neck. It was erotic and intoxicating. The sensation shot straight to her clit.

Maggie straightened and smiled, her dimples showing. "I came to you because I couldn't let you think in here…" She pointed to her chest, Rayne chose to believe she was pointing to her heart. "I was the cold, heartless person that walked away last night." Maggie was no longer smiling. The teasingly seductive tone had left, too.

The world fell away. In an instant, she forgot they were in her office and caressed Maggie's cheek, then cupped her chin. "Listen to me." She spoke softly. Their eyes met once more. "You haven't done anything wrong. I think we're both suffering the effects of our fears and the unknown."

Maggie's mouth opened. Before any words came out, Rayne touched a finger to her lips, quieting her.

"I think it's really sweet that you came to my office to tell me, but we can't do this here." There was a look of disappointment that flashed across Maggie's face as she backed away.

"Of course. I don't know what I was thinking." Maggie turned to leave. Rayne caught her wrist.

"Can we talk more tonight?" she said, then remembered what was in the refrigerator. "I have leftovers from a wonderful restaurant."

Maggie laughed, and her expression went from somber to relaxed. "Oh, you do? Well, that's an offer I can't refuse." She smiled. "I'll see you tonight."

Then she was gone. Rayne was left dumbfounded and confused. *What just happened?* Before she could sort out the mix of emotions, her phone rang.

"Hello. This is Rayne."

The voice was one she wished she didn't recognize. "Dr. Thomas, it's Dana in the research office. Mr. Carmichael needs to see you. Please bring a copy of your latest effort report."

Shit! What was going on today? At this rate, she wasn't going to get to work on her paper until after lunch, and she still had to create a schedule for repeating the experiments that had given her results that would further her career if she could duplicate them. She gathered her tablet and a pad of paper before heading out the door. As she rushed past Deb, she gave her a quick update. "Urgent meeting with Carmichael. I have no idea how long I'll be."

Deb stood and handed her a to-go cup of steaming coffee. "Whatever it is, it'll be fine."

Rayne held up the cup. "Thanks." She stepped on the elevator as the doors shut, ushering her up to the administrative research office on the eighth floor of the building. She blew into the lidded cup and sipped. It was the perfect temperature for drinking. Luckily for her, she and Deb liked their coffee the same way.

Whatever was so urgent, she was in no mood for jumping through hoops. She smoothed a hand over her pants and straightened her sweater before the number eight lit up. A deep breath would go a long way in helping her face whatever dilemma awaited her.

CHAPTER TWENTY-SEVEN

More than an hour later, Rayne walked lightly over the tiled foyer in her Sketchers. Deb looked up expectantly. "Anything need the fire department down here?"

Deb signaled all was clear. "You survived."

"I'd swear off technology if I didn't need it to help interpret results. *Someone* screwed up all the effort reporting in my documents. We had to go over them all with a fine-tooth comb and compare what I had originally reported with what showed in the database." She snagged a snickerdoodle from the tray on Deb's raised counter. "I blame the new guy." Not everyone was proficient at the statistical reporting system. Hell, she was barely able to figure out what number needed to go where. But still, Maggie's visit and the latest "emergency" had cost her most of the morning. Using her time wisely was not only smart, but it was also paramount in her job. It was time she got on with her original plans for the day, productivity-wise.

"Now that the latest system hiccup is rectified, I'm going to park at my desk, head down, and map out an experimental sequence before lunch." It sounded good in theory anyway.

"Want me to order in? Then you won't have to break your concentration." There was a reason Deb was looked at as the "go-to" of the department. Forward thinking. Every research entity needed a Deb.

"Excellent idea. You pick, my treat." Rayne relied on Deb to order something that would be consumable with one hand, leaving the other to write or type. A working lunch where she actually got to eat wasn't possible at the bench, but it happened frequently in her office. The mini fridge was stocked with beverages and one side of the credenza held an array of soups, side dishes, and non-perishables.

Rayne passed the small mirror hanging over the credenza, glanced at her reflection, and stopped. Her hair was a mess from repeatedly running her fingers through it while she tried to make sense of the spreadsheet that spanned two monitors on Josh's desk. It had boggled her mind when she first sat down, like she was looking at a foreign species, unable to decipher what was up or down, right or left. While a lot of people in her field worked with multiple monitors, even the idea of having to scroll back and forth, clicking on one screen then jumping to another, made her head spin. At one point, he ran his hand over his face and looked at her.

"I have no right to take my frustrations out on you, Rayne. I'm sorry." He gave her an apologetic smile, and though it was tight, she appreciated the effort. "If you weren't so meticulous with your recordkeeping, we'd have no idea how to fix this."

The compliment was a boost to her ego, and she took a moment to enjoy the pride of knowing her painstaking compulsion for details sometimes paid off. Rayne dropped into her chair and sank into its soft padding. She took five minutes to do some deep breathing, then pulled out her lab notebook, a clean pad of paper, and the results of her experiment in chart and graph form. Rayne delved in, comforted by the fact she had a destination and a goal, and an idea how to get there. All she had to do was put it down on paper.

Almost three hours later, there was a rap on her door, followed by an arm holding a paper bag. She set her pencil down and laughed.

"Is it safe for the rest of me?" Deb asked tentatively.

"It is. Especially if there's food." She glanced at the tiny numbers at the bottom of her screen. It was just past one in the afternoon. No wonder she was hungry.

Deb opened the door all the way, smiling. She placed the bag on the corner of Rayne's desk. "How's it going?"

She went to the fridge and pulled out a bottle of flavored water. She'd been so wrapped up in her work she hadn't drank anything since sitting down. She cracked the seal. It was cold and refreshing. "It's slow going, but I want to be sure I have all the steps outlined for a successful replication of the first experiment."

"Can anyone help?" Deb sat in the only other chair there was room for.

That was a question she'd been mulling over for the last hour. Whoever Rayne involved in the experiment, she had to be sure she could trust them to be as meticulous as she was with the sequence of events and collection of the data. "Mark is a really focused student. He might be up for the challenge." Part of her job was to teach the students in the lab about protocol, theory, and interpreting data. She couldn't do that if they never had the opportunity to prove they had what it took to be a scientist. Before she talked with Mark she wanted Steve's opinion. He was much better at knowing a student's potential than she was.

"He's just starting his second year. Do you think he's capable?" Deb knew everyone in the department not only by name, but also their strengths and weaknesses. Some day when she had toughened her inner shell, she was going to ask Deb for an assessment of hers.

Rayne shrugged as she chewed the bite of chicken salad on pumpernickel with bibb lettuce and sharp cheddar. "He's shown interest in the project and asked a lot of questions. If he gets stuck, he'll ask for help or discuss the possible implications. If there's someone else who can do a better job, I haven't seen them yet."

Deb was quiet while Rayne listed the pros and cons in her head. That white board was getting full and needed to be wiped clean soon. "Looks like you already made your decision." Deb stood.

She glanced up at her. "You might be right."

"I'm always right, but I don't always say so." Deb lifted her brow, the ghost of a smile on her mouth. "You'll know what to do."

With the science, Rayne didn't have a doubt. What she was going to do about Maggie and their shared desire to have sex was a horse of a different color.

❖

"Why are you so nervous?" Jill asked, her brows knit in concern.

"I'm not." Maggie had been on edge since arriving at work, her mind back at the lab where Rayne worked. "It's been a long day."

"You've had them before. What gives?"

Maggie blew out her breath. She needed to talk to someone about her mixed emotions. She wasn't sure Jill was the right person, but she didn't have a lot of options. "You know Rayne and I are friends, right?"

Jill stared at her. "So you've said."

She had. Probably too often for anyone to believe that's all they were. "I like her. It's been hard to connect with anyone since Eve." During a night of beer and dares, Maggie had told Jill the story of her first love and how shattered she'd been when Eve died. "I don't let people get close, and I think I'm over that."

"You're ready to move on." Jill's features softened and she put her hand on Maggie's arm and gently squeezed. "That's a good thing."

"I know, it's just…" She looked away. "I'm not sure I remember how to be a girlfriend."

"That's what's got you so twisted?"

Maggie nodded. Twisted was a perfect description of her gut every time she tried to figure out how she was going to explain why she'd been so hot and cold to Rayne. "We haven't been together, together." Fuck. This was hard.

"You mean you haven't been intimate?"

"Right. That." She pulled her fingers through her hair.

Jill straddled the bench and motioned her to do the same. "And that's something you want?"

"Yes. No. Shit. I do, but that's not all. I need connection, too, and laughing and silliness."

"And sex." Jill said it plainly.

"Yeah. And I'm scrambling to make sense of how to say what I'm feeling that won't make Rayne think I'm a lunatic, or worse." She stood with her hands on her hips.

"So, what's your plan so she doesn't think that?" Jill understood her predicament, which was a bit of a comfort.

"We're going to talk tonight. I've tried to rehearse what I want to say, but every time I try it out loud, it sounds worse than the time before." She blew out a long breath. Any relationship was only as good as the sum of its parts. Some of its parts were rough around the edges and needed to be smoothed. Others brought a lot of baggage that both parties needed to make peace with. Maggie sat down again.

Jill placed her hand on her thigh. "Try not to worry so much. I'm sure you'll get the point across no matter how it comes out." She stood. "I'm happy for you, Maggie. It's time you planted roots and nurtured them."

There was a small part of her that believed Jill, though the most important part of tonight was putting her feelings out on the table to examine them, but not just hers. Rayne also had to have an equal amount of airtime. Dating was hard. Harder still was not fucking up a good thing, and she and Rayne were off the charts.

Rayne glanced at the clock and groaned. Her back hurt and she rubbed the spot that was sore from being first hunched over her lab notes, then at the bench doing the legwork of an experiment that involved counting cells grown in culture medium. The cells would be injected into her test subjects and, if the results matched the prior experiment, she could write a paper. In turn, it would supply the basis of taking the theory further with the support of a federal grant.

She rubbed my eyes and stood. "That's it. The rest will have to wait till morning," she said out loud as she put the petri dishes back in storage. Inside her cramped office, Rayne gathered her messenger bag and purse as she shut down the desktop computer. The halls were quiet, the lights in the main office dim. Everyone was long gone. She closed the door behind her as exhaustion coursed through her body. All she wanted was a hot shower and a glass of wine. *Shit! Maggie! They were supposed to have dinner tonight. Damnit!* She'd have to hurry, or else Maggie would be standing outside her door. The elevators were especially slow. While she waited, she checked her phone and panic rose when she saw she'd missed a message from Maggie.

Hey, Rayne. Hope you're having a good day. I have to cover Larry's seven o'clock class. I'm sorry for the late notice. Give me a call when you get this.

Thank the gods. If everything was in her favor, she'd have a little over an hour to whip up a dessert, shower, and dress before Maggie showed. The good news was that she was fifteen minutes from work, and she prayed it would be enough.

Once in the car, she pressed the speed dial number. While it rang she leaned her head back and rubbed the tension from her neck. She really needed that hot shower.

"Hi." Maggie's soft voice answered.

"Hi, Mags. Everything okay with Larry?" Rolling her neck and shoulders made the bones crack and pop, sounding like breakfast cereal.

"He's fine. He thinks one of his kids gave him the crud. The class just ended." She laughed a bit. "You still at work?"

Rayne started the car and her Bluetooth kicked in. "Just leaving. I need a hot shower and a masseuse." It was the truth.

"Have you eaten?" Maggie asked, sounding concerned.

"Not since lunch." Had it been that long ago?

Maggie sighed into the phone. "You have to eat."

She pulled onto the highway. In ten minutes, she'd be home. "Honestly, I don't have the energy."

"I have an idea. I could meet you at your place. You take as long a shower as you need, and I'll heat up the leftovers. That way you can relax. And if you like, I could give you a massage after dinner."

One side of her brain set off flares and rockets with the warning, "Bad, bad idea." The softer side, the side that found Maggie attractive and someone she enjoyed spending time with, was jumping up and down yelling, "Yes, yes!" Tired of useless self-denial, she gave in to the softer side.

"That sounds perfect, but what about you?"

"What about me?

"You worked all day, too."

"I'm fine. I'd really like to do this for you."

"Uh...really?"

"Yes, really."

Rayne relaxed with the idea of being pampered for a change. "Okay."

Maggie's smile came through in her voice. "Great. I'm going to shower. I'll see you soon."

The line went dead. "Bye, Mags," she whispered. Her heart raced wildly in her chest. *What did I agree to?*

For the remainder of her ride home, Rayne argued with her conscience. On the one hand, she didn't want to take advantage of Maggie's generosity. The other hand, the one that often left her feeling alone and isolated, held on to a glimmer of hope that tonight would lead to something more. Terrified and elated at the same time, Rayne pressed the pedal harder, intent on getting home before Maggie arrived.

Five minutes after racing through the door, Rayne shoved a blueberry pie into the oven, the edge of the crust wrapped in aluminum foil. She'd have Maggie pull it off when there was fifteen minutes left on the timer. Luckily, she had a ready-to-bake pie in the freezer, allowing her to avoid looking as unprepared as she felt. The idea of a crisp, fruity white wine sounded like the perfect accompaniment, but if they ended up having a serious conversation she wanted a clear head, so as much as she wanted it, the bottle would stay tucked in the fridge, at least until they were done. In the meantime, she could offer sparkling water, tea, or coffee. The doorbell rang, and her pulse quickened.

❖

"Hi. I brought wine." Maggie held up two bottles of white.

"I was going to abstain." She opened the door wider. "But since you came to tempt me, I'm not sure I can." She headed to the kitchen with Maggie on her heels.

"You don't have to have any if you don't want to." Maggie set the bottles down, clearly waiting for her cue.

She pulled two glasses from the cabinet and turned. "And miss out on your impeccable selections? Not a chance."

Maggie cracked the seal and filled their glasses, then handed one to Rayne. "To a great way of starting the weekend. Cheers." After a sip, Maggie took Rayne's hand and pulled her along down the hall, making Rayne giggle.

"Take as long as you want in the shower," Maggie said with a serious face. "Maybe you should think about a bath instead."

Rayne opened her mouth to protest, but Maggie wasn't going to let her.

"That was the deal. I cook, you relax."

Something in the heated glint of Maggie's eyes got her moving. Rayne was afraid if she stood there any longer, Maggie was going to either touch her or kiss her. As much as she wanted both, she wasn't ready for either. At the last second, she called over her shoulder, "Take the foil off the pie when the buzzer sounds, then put it back in for fifteen."

"Got it," Maggie called as she closed the bedroom door. Rayne considered the suggestion of a bath, but she was sure she'd fall asleep, so she settled for a steaming shower. She dropped her clothes in the hamper and snagged a shower bomb before entering. The aromatic scent of jasmine and honeysuckle rose to meet her. The combination of heat and scent soothed her tired body. The lavender soap added another layer of calm. When she emerged ten minutes later, her eyes were heavy, her body relaxed. Her bed called to her. It would have been nice to crawl into bed. Instead, she pulled on her favorite robe and slippers, wanting to finish her wine before she dressed. Rayne opened the door to the sound of Maggie softly singing along with music playing from someplace.

"It smells good in here."

Maggie turned and a slow smile spread across her lips. "Feel better?"

"Much. Thank you." She watched Maggie move about with fluid ease. Of course, they'd been to each other's homes a half-dozen times and it was no surprise she knew her way around. The scene was a flash of what a future with Maggie might look like. Or maybe it was just her hopeful imagination this was how it could be. Maggie stood with her back to her, and she drank in the view of her lean, carved figure. Muscles flexed as she moved. Reaching, and her biceps bulged. A step, and the material covering her thigh went taut. She had to get out of there before she did something stupid. She threw back the last of her wine. When she started to turn, the room dipped, and she grabbed the edge of the counter.

"Whoa. You okay?" Maggie wrapped her arm around Rayne's waist, steadying her.

Rayne sank against Maggie for a brief moment before breaking contact. "I'm fine." She wasn't fine at all. She wanted to give in to the urge to drag Maggie to her bedroom and make her fantasies come true.

There was doubt written on Maggie's face. She took a step away and leaned against the breakfast bar, crossing her arms in front of her. "Really?"

Rayne gathered her wits and took a breath. "I might be a bit dehydrated." It was as good an excuse as any.

Maggie went to the pantry, brought out an open bottle of water, and helped her to a stool. "Take some slow sips." The buzzer sounded and she hesitated.

"Don't you dare let that pie burn." She forced her voice to sound stronger than she felt.

With her task done, Maggie returned to her and knelt at her side. "How do you feel?"

She didn't want to start tonight with lies. Not tonight or any night with Maggie. She wasn't the type of person who would want to be lied to with the idea of sparing her pain. Rayne had a feeling she already knew pain and had walked through it. "Better. I need to go get clothes on for dinner."

"I think you look great." The heat in Maggie's eyes made her heart skip a beat.

"Thanks, but no." She stood slowly. When the world stayed level, she smiled. "But don't expect a fashion show. It's loungewear all the way."

"Sounds perfect." Maggie returned to the kitchen. "By the time you get back dinner will be served.

"Now *that* sounds perfect to me."

CHAPTER TWENTY-EIGHT

C ertain leftovers taste even better the second time around," Rayne said as she sat back in her chair, the last of the wine in her glass.

"That's true." Maggie stood and began clearing dishes.

"I've got this, you cooked," Rayne said.

She snorted. "I tossed leftovers in the microwave and did what you said for the pie. That's hardly cooking."

"I'm stuffed and relaxed, so I'm not going to fight you on this as long as you promise to put the dishes in the dishwasher."

Once she was in the kitchen and out of earshot, Maggie let go of all she'd been holding inside. "Fuck. That woman has no idea how hot she is," she mumbled under her breath. She scraped the meager remnants of food into the garbage and rinsed the dishes. She'd never really gotten the hang of stacking a dishwasher efficiently, but the one Rayne had was large and well-configured without the weird-shaped racks that made it difficult to tell what went where. It didn't hurt that there was a picture on the door.

The coffee was set to go. The delicious-looking pie sat on the counter. She pressed her fingers to the plate and was pleased it was still warm. The mugs were next to the sugar and empty creamer pitcher. Her stomach was pleasantly full, too, but the idea of coffee and pie would win over reason at some point. In the meantime, she filled two glasses with crushed ice and water from the dispenser.

Maggie found Rayne tucked into a corner of the couch. Her eyes were closed, but she didn't think she was sleeping. "Rayne?" she said after setting the glasses down.

"Hmmm?" Rayne's eyes slowly opened. "Sorry. I might have dozed off."

"We should talk." She wasn't looking forward to having the conversation she was about to have with Rayne, but it needed to be said and she promised herself she wouldn't stall anymore.

"I know." Rayne looked down at her hands. "I don't know where to start."

"I think it should be me. You've told me about Heather and the breakup. I haven't said much about Eve, other than she died." Even after eight years of missing her, the knot in Maggie's throat returned. Rayne reached for her but didn't touch her.

"You don't have to. I can see it still hurts."

She shook her head. "It's time I tell it. No one's heard the whole story and I want to tell you. You just can't…if you touch me, I won't be able to finish."

Rayne slid her hand away. "Okay." She backed into the corner of the couch to face her.

"From the time I was a youngster I was into sports. Anything and everything my parents would let me do. And even some they didn't." She laughed at memory of the shock on her mom's face when she showed up with a black eye after playing "boxer" with one of the neighborhood boys. She only found out later he had two black eyes, but Maggie could have sworn there was a bit of admiration on her face when she did. "By the time I got to high school I was a typical teenaged jock and enjoyed the high of pushing my physical limits. Then there was a car accident."

Rayne's hand covered her mouth. Maybe she was trying to suppress asking questions.

"We were all fine in the end. I broke my arm and was in a cast for almost two months. The doctor assured me it would be as good as ever. I asked what kind of a doctor he was. When he told me he was a sports medicine doctor it didn't take me long to make up my mind that's what I wanted to be."

Rayne began to squirm. "I'm sorry. I really need the bathroom." She jumped up.

Maybe now was a good time to start the coffee. She could use the break to gather her thoughts. Rayne took her spot on the couch. "I turned on the coffee maker."

"So, sports medicine?"

"Yeah. I had it all planned out. By the time I was twenty-six, I'd be ready to practice. I met Eve in my freshman year of college." Visions of a bright-eyed, bubbly Eve flashed in front of her. "She was going to be a physical therapist, so we were in a few classes together. She was a bit of a jock herself, but in a feminine way. I thought that was pretty hot back then."

"You don't anymore?"

"Not in the same way I thought I did." Eve was special. A one of a kind who stole Maggie's heart without her even knowing it for a while. "At the beginning of our second year, her stamina wasn't what it had been. She blamed the crazy courseload. It was a reasonable assumption. Everyone was exhausted all the time." Maybe she should have noticed something, but what did she know? She had just finished two sixteen-credit semesters. Eve wasn't the only one who was tired. Maggie questioned her own ability to tough out two more semesters with a similar load. The coffee beeped. As much as she wanted the energy boost, she wanted to finish this more. Rayne must have noticed her hesitation.

"It'll keep."

She nodded, took a breath, and made eye contact. "She liked to run when she was stressed. One morning before our first class, she came by my dorm to let me know she'd meet me there. Two hours later, Eve didn't show. Twenty minutes after that, a sinking feeling settled in my gut. I sent her a text. Nothing. I was on the verge of panic, but I came up with a dozen reasons why she hadn't shown and was late for class. It wasn't until class was almost over that someone slid next to me and told me my roommate was looking for me. Sheila and I weren't enemies, but we weren't chummy, either." She'd raced back to her building and Sheila was waiting in the common room. So was Eve's roommate. They'd both been crying.

"Oh, Maggie."

"That's when I found out Eve had a massive heart attack while running. By the time someone found her, it was too late."

"I'm going to touch you now." Rayne sat next to her and wrapped her arm around her shoulders. She didn't realize she was crying until Rayne wiped her tears away.

"You loved her."

"Yeah. Neither one of us said the words, but I knew, and I think Eve loved me, too." A fresh wave of pain hit. "She died without hearing it. Three words. That's all I had to say." She looked into Rayne's eyes. "I never want to feel that way again."

Rayne thumbed away the last tears. "I don't think you will. The next time you fall in love you'll say them. When you feel them, you'll say them, and you won't have to carry the guilt eating your insides anymore."

She took another shaky breath and hoped Rayne understood what she'd been trying to tell her, but she had to be sure. "The push and pull. The uncertainty. I've been afraid of the feelings I have when I'm with you. Afraid that if we're more than friends, there might be a day when I hesitate to say the words again."

"You can't know that, Mags. No one knows the future." Rayne kissed her cheek. "Besides, I think you're getting ahead of yourself."

"What do you mean?"

"We haven't officially dated very long." Rayne ducked her head. "Or had sex. You might suck at being a lover."

Shock rippled through her. Then Rayne began to giggle, and the weight of her confession lifted. "You're a jerk." She stood to get coffee. "I don't suck at sex."

Disappointment settled into Rayne's features. "That's too bad," she said as she followed her into the kitchen. "I was rather hoping you did." She went to the cupboard and brought out bowls and plates. "I enjoy a good sucking."

Funny how Rayne was the one giving her the confidence to try to love again, and she was right. If they weren't sexually compatible they'd need to reexamine their feelings. As much as people pretended sex between partners didn't matter because they loved each other, they didn't call it lesbian bed death for nothing, even if it was a myth.

Chapter Twenty-nine

Rayne drifted awake to the sound of the television. Behind it were the soft snores from Maggie beside her. They'd gotten through coffee and dessert and settled on a series they both wanted to watch. She glanced at the clock and was surprised at how long she'd been asleep. As quietly as possible, she gathered the plates and cups. After rinsing, she put them in the dishwasher, smiling at the unorthodox stacking Maggie had done. Her heart ached at Maggie's story of losing her lover. She couldn't imagine what that would be like, and she hoped never to find out. Maggie's sharing had been emotionally charged and not in a good way. She had no intention of waking her.

"That's my job," Maggie said from behind her.

"Hey." She went to Maggie as she leaned against the archway. "How are you feeling?"

"Okay." Maggie glanced at her socks with barbells on them. "Sorry I zonked out on you."

Her head was telling her to keep her distance. "You didn't." She lightly twined their fingers. "I fell asleep, too."

"It's late. I should probably go." She looked at their joined hands, then tried to move away,

Rayne put her free hand on her chest. "Stay." Her heart beat like a drum. Deep. Strong.

"You don't know what you're asking." Maggie's fingertips brushed her cheek.

"Yes, I do."

"I can't sleep on the couch. I can't have you so close and so far."

She held Maggie's hand in place. "Who said anything about a couch?" She took Maggie not running for the door as a good sign and led her down the hallway to her bedroom, much the same way Maggie had led her a few hours ago. Even though she knew Maggie had been with other women, she needed this time, with her, to be different. To feel different for both of them. Rayne crawled onto the bed, clothes on, hoping Maggie followed. She wanted to go slow and enjoy what might be the only time they were together. She didn't have a crystal ball foretelling the future. All she had was hope and she prayed it was enough.

Is this really happening? Maggie had thought about how it might go. How she'd try not to anticipate how dating Rayne might feel. What her own reaction would be when she finally made love to someone she cared about for more than a quick romp. Rayne lay down on the bed. Watching. Waiting. She'd jerked her around enough. First by suggesting she date even when she cringed when she did and became distraught when she watched women at the lounge look at her like they wanted her naked and…no, she didn't need to go there. Rayne had left with her. Rayne spent time with her.

She watched as Rayne lifted the edge of her shirt, revealing her creamy, pale skin beneath. An obvious attempt to lure her into joining her. What was it going to take to settle the butterflies she tried to ignore all day and then again during dinner? She didn't want to be dressed when she lay down next to Rayne. *Let her lead.* The voice was soft but clear. She settled on her side before running her hand over Rayne's hip, then over her thigh.

"I don't want to put you in an awkward position." Rayne touched her face. Her hand drifted to her neck, then the place above her breast.

"You aren't." She formed a half-smile. "I can be awkward all on my own."

Rayne softly chuckled. "It becomes you."

"Really? You like a woman who questions everything she does?" She hadn't meant to let the words out and prayed she'd only heard them in her own head.

"I don't want you to question anything when it comes to us."

Apparently she'd spoken out loud.

"Tell me what you're feeling."

What could she say? Would what came out of her mouth be anything like the emotions coursing through her brain? Or the pounding of her heart? Or the heat pooling between her thighs? She leaned close until there was barely any space between her and Rayne, then she pressed her lips to Rayne's. Gently at first. As the seconds passed and her need for more rose, she took what she wanted. Needed. Maggie pressed her tongue and Rayne's mouth opened to her. The moan that escaped spoke volumes, and still she craved more.

"I want you naked for me." It wasn't a request nor a demand. It was simply stated. Maggie waited for Rayne to show her she wanted to be naked *for* her.

On her knees, Rayne's gaze held hers as she pulled off her top. The black camisole layer beneath did little to hide her chest. When that layer was removed, Rayne's full breasts beckoned to be touched. Her fingers twitched as she looked from them to Rayne's eyes. "Magnificent." Rayne's cheeks flushed pink. She pressed her lips to Rayne's mouth and when she opened to let her in, Maggie sank into the sweet flavor while she explored. By the time she backed away, they were both breathless.

Rayne smiled. "That was hot."

"Yeah."

"You're overdressed." Rayne lifted the edge of her shirt slowly, pressing her lips to her exposed skin. She stopped when she freed her breasts, made eye contact, then slipped her lips around her nipple and sucked.

A shiver of excitement traveled down her spine. "Rayne." The name sounded like a prayer, a call to a higher power.

"Mmm." Rayne lifted her shirt all the way off and tossed it on the chair. Her eyes twinkled with glee. "I'll finish undressing you, if you finish undressing me."

Her clit beat between her swollen folds. Being turned on so much so quickly was a new experience for her. Maggie was used to not only leading the way, but setting the pace while holding back until she was ready for more. Rayne taking the lead was unexpected. She untied the string on Rayne's lounge pants, hooked her fingers inside the material, and pulled, only to groan out loud when nothing but the pale skin of Rayne's abdomen came into view. "That's so unfair."

Rayne unbuttoned Maggie's jeans with a quick twist of her wrist. "What's unfair is you seeing all of me when you're still half hidden." She made short work of getting Maggie naked. All of Rayne's fantasizing couldn't compare with the sight before her. Maggie was lean and muscular in all the right places. A lush display of trim, dark brown hair surrounded her slit, and she was mesmerized by the drops of moisture that clung to them. Rayne swung her leg over her hip and straddled her. "I've thought about this happening ever since the dream, but I wasn't prepared for how much my imagination fell short when it came to seeing your body."

Maggie's hands slid up her sides, and she pulled her closer. "I could say the same thing," she said, smiling.

"I wasn't sure. The other night when you left, I thought it was because you didn't know how to tell me you weren't interested in more than that kiss. The idea you'd been wrong in your feelings—"

"Are you crazy?" Maggie held her. "I had all I could do not to tackle you. It might have been hard to tell at the time, but I have always been attracted to you. Not just because of your sexy body either. All of you, Rayne."

"But you walked out and..." Rayne couldn't finish. The disappointment she'd felt was still fresh in her mind.

"Because I didn't want to take advantage of a situation where you might have felt vulnerable." Maggie studied her. "You—we—both gave mixed signals."

"Are there mixed signals now?" She rubbed her center against Maggie's, the dampness mingling with her own.

"No." Maggie's voice caught in her throat, but she understood her well enough.

"And," she said before taking one nipple into her mouth, sucking in as much of her breast as she could manage, "how about now?" She wanted Maggie to surrender to the moment. To reveal how much they mistakenly ignored the signs of the depth of their desire.

Maggie flipped Rayne to her back. Not leading might have been an intoxicating notion, but she wasn't about to totally abandon who she was, and who she was meant taking control. "There are a lot of reasons for the mixed messages, but if I didn't think you were worth all the fussing, I wouldn't have come back. Try not to doubt that." She palmed Rayne's face.

"I'll try to remember." The smile on Rayne's lips was genuine.

"Good." Maggie looked along their bodies wondering how two people could fit together so perfectly. Sure, she wanted to do things with and to her, but the wonder of finally feeling all of Rayne against her held its own awe.

"Maggie?" Rayne asked as she lightly scored her back with her short nails.

"Yes?" She traced the line of Rayne's jaw, down her neck, between her breasts, raising gooseflesh and making her shiver.

"Are you going to touch me soon, because if you don't, I'm pretty sure I'll go crazy."

Maggie slipped her hand between them and found Rayne's soft mound wet and her clit hard. She gently rubbed the knot, teasing it to respond. "Like this?" she asked before she kissed Rayne's plump lips. Rayne moaned into her mouth. "Or this?" Her fingers were coated with Rayne's essence as they entered her hot hole. This time, she was the one who moaned. "Fuck. You're so ready, baby."

"God, yes." Rayne pressed upward, opening herself fully to her strokes. "I'm not going to last long." Rayne became incredibly wetter.

"Let's slow down." Maggie was ready too, and the thought of this being her first and only time to touch Rayne, to watch her surrender to her touches, sent her into panic mode. She started to back out. Rayne held her hand in place.

"Don't." Rayne's insides tightened around her fingers. "Please, please don't stop."

What was she to do? Rayne's hazy eyes pleaded, matching her words. "Let go, babe." Maggie leaned closer and kissed her firmly. She thumbed Rayne's clit between pumps and without warning, Rayne broke the kiss and groaned, bucking against her hard. She watched the transformation of her face as Rayne's orgasm ripped through her. Deep, soulful whimpers followed. After she slipped out, she painted Rayne's lips with her own essence. The best lip gloss she'd ever seen enticed her to kiss her again.

Rayne's doe-like eyes studied her. "I couldn't stop if I'd wanted to."

Maggie smiled. "I didn't want you to stop. I wanted you to enjoy what was happening."

"Oh, I did, and I hope you could tell."

She pulled Rayne into her arms, the need to snuggle after giving her pleasure a feeling she'd not had in a very long time. "It was amazing to watch you come." She kissed her forehead. "Thank you."

Rayne's gaze turned upward. "You don't have to thank me, but you do have to give me the same pleasure." She moved and straddled her thigh, the wet heat of Rayne's center coating her skin. Her hands moved along Maggie's abdomen, her ribs, over her arms. "You're as sculpted naked as I imagined you'd be." She pressed her lips between her breasts. "Even better."

Rayne plucked her nipples with just the right pressure and Maggie sucked air between her teeth. When Rayne's lips closed over one and gently sucked, moisture trickled from her center and her excitement grew. Then Rayne's mouth was on hers, her tongue outlined her lips before teasing to enter, and she gladly welcomed her in. Lost in sensation, she stayed in the moment. She had wondered if she'd ever find someone to make her feel as deeply as she did right then.

Rayne's hazy gaze met hers before she slowly slid down the length of her body and settled between her legs. "Is this okay?"

Desire coursed through Maggie. It had been a long time since she'd relaxed and enjoyed being on the receiving end of attention. She wasn't about to let the opportunity pass. "It's very okay."

Rayne smiled against her flesh as she slid her arms around her thighs, drawing her closer. "I've been imagining you taste like honey." Rayne's tongue slipped between her slippery folds and the first swipe sent a shiver of anticipation in every direction. "Mmm. I was right."

Maggie watched while Rayne's mouth and tongue did a magical dance against her sensitive flesh. Her clit began to beat in earnest, and an inner dialogue of wanting to wait while wanting to relent to the rhythmic strokes ensued.

"Get out of your head and let go," Rayne said, as though knowing she was at war with her emotions. Rayne moved her hand upward and squeezed her nipple, sending shock waves directly to her center.

The buildup of her impending orgasm steadily overtook all thoughts and Maggie went with it, luxuriating in the intensity as her legs began to tremble. The more she shook, the tighter Rayne hung on, her tongue painting her flesh as though she was a beloved canvas and Rayne was the artist bringing it to life. She ached to hold on a little longer, but she couldn't. With an arch in her back, she hung on mere seconds then exploded with a roar as she stiffened. She rode the pinnacle of her climax. Ecstasy drove her deeper into the bliss until she collapsed onto the bed, her chest heaving and her center pulsing so hard against Rayne's hungry mouth she came again before everything outside of her body ceased to exist.

CHAPTER THIRTY

Rayne had drawn the sheet over them and nestled against Maggie's chest. She'd never seen anyone orgasm the way Maggie had with her clit pounding against her tongue and her entire body shaking in the aftermath of the second one that came before the first had subsided. Maggie's release had been exquisite, and Rayne couldn't help feeling gratified. After all, she was well aware of some of the women Maggie had slept with. They were all beautiful in some way. But then she remembered that Heather had been a beauty, yet she'd kept Rayne around for a long time. Rayne thought she was a decent lover, but after seeing Maggie's reaction, maybe she had bragging rights. She giggled. One session didn't make her a Don Juan in bed, but it was nice to dream. She flicked her gaze upward as Maggie began to stir. When her eyes slowly opened, she smiled.

"Hi."

Maggie groaned. "What did you do to me?" She laughed weakly.

"Uh…licked your clit."

"Fuck. You certainly did." Maggie drew her closer. "You have a magical tongue."

"Thank you. You're sweet."

"I'm think I'm more of a limp noodle."

She laughed. "No. I meant you taste sweet."

"Oh." Maggie ran her hand over her face. "Good to know."

"In all the situations I've seen you in, I've never seen you embarrassed."

Maggie scooted until her back was against the headboard. "Yeah, well, I've never felt the earth fall away until tonight, so I think we're even." Her laugh turned into a cough.

Rayne grabbed a bottle of water off the nightstand and handed it to her. "I got us a drink while you dozed."

Maggie cracked the seal and drank half before responding. "Passed out is more like it."

"Potato, patato," she said. "You're okay though, right?" For all of her bragging she hadn't thought to make sure Maggie was mentally okay.

"It might be a bit before I can walk, but I'm fine."

"Good. That's good." She chewed on her lower lip, unsure where things stood between them. The silence wasn't exactly uncomfortable, but it did feel like they were in an awkward place. Maybe if they were dressed, it would be easier to talk. "I'm in need of wine and a snack." She slipped from under the covers and slowly searched for her clothes, not wanting to give the impression that she was in a hurry to escape.

"That's a great idea." Maggie started searching the floor.

"I tossed most of your things on the chair."

Maggie picked up a dark scrap of material and held them out. "These have to be yours."

"Thanks." After she snatched the little lace bikini bottoms, she laughed. "I have no idea where my bra ended up."

"You had a bra?" Maggie's brow rose. "I have no memory of a bra."

"Lot of help you are." She pulled on her T-shirt and decided the rest could wait. "Come on. Let's get some sustenance before we wither away." Rayne padded to the kitchen with Maggie not far behind. She rummaged in the refrigerator and pulled a bottle of Matua Sauvignon Blanc from the back of a shelf. Then she added a bunch of green grapes, sharp cheese, and a box of wheat crackers.

"What else?" Maggie stood with her hands on her hips. She'd found her pants and shirt. She was barefoot and Rayne suspected she hadn't found her bra because her nipples were poking at the material.

"Glasses, small plates, and some napkins."

"On it." Maggie respectfully searched until she located the items.

"Can you take them to the living room and find something on TV that won't require deep thinking?"

"I can."

With a minute to herself, Rayne tried to gather her thoughts. She wasn't about to let the night end without knowing where they were headed. The last time something important was left to chance, they'd suffered a needless misunderstanding. The flirting, then withdrawing, had only led to guessing games. That behavior had seen its day. They were adults and could talk about their feelings. She sliced the cheese and tossed the small wooden board on a tray along with the rest of the items.

"How mindless do you want to go? Like *Naked and Afraid* mindless, or more like endless reruns of *Friends*?"

"*Friends* for sure. I just get pissed off that people on *Naked* are so stupid." She set the tray down, cracked open the wine, and poured. After handing one to Maggie, she toasted. "To not being naked and afraid."

"Hear, hear. I'll drink to that." Maggie sipped, smiled, and crossed her long legs at the ankles.

They sat in relative silence except for laughing at some antic on TV and occasionally grabbing a piece of cheese or a cracker. Her thoughts wouldn't quiet, and her anxiety grew. "What's next?"

Maggie pressed a button on the remote and scrolled. "Season five, episode three." Sometimes she was clueless.

"With us, Mags. What's next for us?"

After she popped a grape in her mouth and chewed, she turned off the volume and faced her. "It's not something we can plan. Going to bed wasn't planned. Not that I haven't thought about it like a trillion times, but I think things that happen naturally..." She shrugged before going on. "Leaves less room for questions."

"Questions?" Maybe she didn't want to know after all.

"You know. The 'what ifs,' or the 'maybe it was too soon.' Or a hundred other worrying thoughts when the moment was perfect, so why think about it except to enjoy the memory?"

It made sense, of course. Maggie was sensible and thoughtful. It was a characteristic that was admirable. She was a different person. "Does that mean we aren't going to discuss it?"

"If that's what you need, we can discuss it as much as you'd like."

"But?" Her gut twisted into a painful knot, and she wondered why she worried so much about Maggie, when she hadn't given her relationship with Heather much thought at all. Light bulb moment.

"It's not necessary." Maggie covered her hand in her larger one. "Did you enjoy earlier?"

Her pulse settled a little. "Absolutely."

Maggie smiled. "So did I. If there's not a problem, it doesn't need picking apart. Right?"

She thought about the philosophy behind her words. Just because her last relationship bombed, didn't mean she needed to get hell-bent on making sure it didn't happen with Maggie, but she was getting way ahead of herself. "I can live with that." She drank wine and focused on what really mattered to her. "I'd like us to date steady."

"You mean exclusively?"

Oh. She hadn't thought otherwise, but maybe she should have. Linguistically, there was a difference. "For now. I think dating leads to commitment at some point. It's not like we have to be attached at the hip. We see each other when we want to. We've spent a lot of time together. I don't think it's too soon to be 'going steady.'" She used air quotes. Did people their age use those terms? She needed to use the Urban Dictionary more often."

Maggie looked as though she were mulling it over and considering the pros and cons as her head tipped from side to side. She moved closer. "Would you please let me take you on a formal date? Show you my chivalrous side?"

She laughed at the formality, but not the implication. "I'd be honored, as long as it doesn't involve hiking, or working out."

"Good." Maggie pecked her cheek, then thumbed her bottom lip. "There. We have a plan, and we know what's next." She poured more wine. "To steady dating and seeing where it leads."

Rayne touched her glass to Maggie's, letting the joyous ring announce the official start of something more. She wasn't a pessimist, but she *was* a realist. Even the best planned experiments didn't always yield the desired results. She hoped this time she'd be pleasantly surprised.

CHAPTER THIRTY-ONE

Y ou look great for having worked late last night." Jill handed Maggie a message from a member stating she wanted a private lesson.

Before last night, Maggie would be looking forward to the hookup, but the news hit differently this morning. She shoved the scrap of paper in the pocket of her shorts on her way to the small kitchen to get a bottle of juice. When she left Rayne's around midnight, she hadn't been able to sleep, tossing and turning until she finally got out of bed and went for a run. She felt a bit better after her shower, but visions of Rayne lingered. "It wasn't too bad. The class was manageable, and the circuits were familiar."

"Good. Don't forget Larry owes you one. He has a tendency to not volunteer even when he's able." Jill looked at the next month's schedule and began filling in names. "Are there any days in particular you want off?"

The date with Rayne needed to be special. One that didn't end with flared tempers or hurt feelings. It would take a little planning on her part, and she'd have to ask Rayne what day would be good for her because she often worked on the weekend, based on her experiments. "Can I get back to you tomorrow?"

Jill held up her pencil. "Sure. This comes with an eraser."

She shook her head. "Everyone's a comedian these days."

"I do what I can." Jill tapped the spreadsheet. "How's things going with Rayne? You don't talk about her much."

How did she want to handle the precarious situation that currently seemed to be on a high note? Jill was the closest person in her life at the moment. Draper was a great cat, but he sucked at both listening and giving constructive feedback. Meowing didn't count. "We've decided to start dating steady."

Jill's head snapped around so quick Maggie was afraid it was going to fly off. "Dating? You?"

Heat infused her cheeks. "Yes me. What? You think I've never dated a woman before?" While it was true since she had started working at the gym all she'd been interested in was a night here or there with an occasional meal thrown in. Nothing steady, and definitely nothing worth talking about.

"Sorry. I just…never mind." Jill studied the sheet again.

Maggie stood in front of the counter and spread her fingers across the paper. "Spill it."

She let out a huff and dropped the pencil. "You're the one who said you hadn't dated since Eve, and with all your cavorting around it wasn't apparent you'd changed your mind. Gee, Maggie, I didn't mean to piss you off."

Her shoulders dropped. Jill was right. "I'm sorry, too. I'm nervous as hell and I don't want to mess this up." She pulled her fingers through her hair. "What do people do on dates these days?"

Jill studied her before bursting out in laughter. When she did, Maggie couldn't help joining her. "I'm pathetic."

"No, you're not. You're out of practice." She picked up her pencil and tapped her chin. "What do you want to do on a date?"

She raised her eyebrows. "Well—"

Jill held her hand out. "Don't say it. What *else* would you like to do on a date?"

"I don't want it to be about me."

"Chivalrous, but after a date or two you'll resent not doing something you enjoy, too."

"Sounds like experience talking," she said.

"Let's not go there. Aside from the gym, what do you enjoy?"

Maggie didn't want to throw things out there off the cuff. "I'm going to hit the treadmill for ten. I think better when my blood is circulating."

"That's sad."

"Hush."

Ten minutes later, she cornered Jill by the water fountain. "Walks by water. Picnics. Lying in a hammock. Outdoor concerts. Festivals. Snuggling by a fire. Paint by number." The seven activities she'd come up with had surprised and delighted her.

"That's an interesting list." Jill sipped from her coffee cup. "Paint by numbers, huh?"

"I happen to have a very light touch and my fine motor skills are great."

"Oh, I'm not doubting your skills at all." She smiled. "Of those, what do you think Rayne would enjoy?"

They hadn't talked a lot about vacations or pastimes. Likely because they both worked a lot. Then she brightened when she remembered a hike they'd taken and the waterfall they'd stopped near for a break. Rayne smiled the entire time. A plan started to form. "A picnic dinner by a little creek that I've passed a hundred times."

"Please tell me you're not going to make her hike on your first going-steady date."

"You make it sound like I don't have a romantic bone in my body." Granted, she'd thought about biking to the spot, but that wouldn't go over well, so she decided to keep it to herself and come up with another way to get there, or somewhere similar. "I'll take care of the details. You make sure whatever day it is I'm off." She went to unlock the front door. "Maybe have me close the next day, too," she said over her shoulder. Jill laughed as she sauntered away.

❖

It had been a bear of a day. First, the central air went out. Then the shipment of membership welcome packages had ended up three hundred miles away at a sister gym. Last, but not least, there'd been a water main break that happened late afternoon. With Jill serving as on-site manager, Maggie had received word that the water should be restored within the next couple of hours, so they'd agreed to stay open. Two hours turned into four, and by the time they were ready to close, she was a stinky, sweaty mess.

Maggie peeled away her clothes and dropped them outside on the balcony, not wanting to deal with them until after she showered. First things first. She adjusted the water to tepid, sparing her body the jolt from being too cold, though the thought of it wasn't unwelcome. With her hair wet enough and after a generous squirt of shampoo, she massaged her scalp as she went and even managed to get some much-needed stimulation with her short nails. This month's body wash was herbal citrus and honey. The scent was fresh and invigorating. By the time she turned the water off, she felt closer to human than she had since midday. Exhausted but refreshed, she dried off and pulled on her favorite sweats and T-shirt. Maggie stuck her feet in her scuffs and went to find something to eat.

As she hit the doorway, Draper meandered up to her, wrapping around Maggie's legs as she walked. She reached down and picked up the wayward cat, scratching his head and behind his ears. Antisocial at times, Draper would sometimes not show for days. The only evidence she had a cat at all was the disappearance of food and the occasional shriek if she forgot to refill his dish. Otherwise, Draper spent his time mousing in the basement or sleeping in some mysterious location. He hated going outside, probably because there had been a few times when Maggie had accidentally left him out all day. On those occasions she would come home to find him screaming at the back door until she let him in.

The refrigerator held a variety of items. Tossed salad, grilled chicken, and steamed vegetables. They were her staples, and she ate some combination of them more often than not. She also had some yogurt, fruit, and sliced turkey. Being low on energy and high on need, she pulled out the chicken and salad. After tossing a piece in the microwave, she filled half her plate with salad, grabbed a flavored seltzer, and added some exotic dressing from one of the little specialty shops downtown. The familiar ding got her moving again. She took her food to the living room and plopped on the couch. It had been days since she'd watched TV. Maybe she should see what was happening in the world.

Her mind wandered while she ate. When was the last time she'd thought about much of anything besides Rayne? It wasn't like her to be unaware of local and world news events that flashed on the screen. For the last two days plans for her date with Rayne had been slowly taking shape. The worry was that what she *thought* Rayne would like might be very different from what she would like, but with the plans in motion she couldn't back out now. Maggie calmed her nervousness by remembering what stage their relationship was in. Plain and simple. She hadn't thought about seeing other women and as far as she knew, neither was Rayne. Maybe it was a bit selfish to think Rayne was ready to take on another relationship. Six months wasn't that long. She might think she was ready to move on, but that point was unproven to some degree. Now who was being a pessimist?

Maggie woke with a start. The TV was on and the gun fight scene in the old-time western was loud enough to wake the dead. *Or the dead asleep.* Grumbling at her stiff body, she turned the TV off as she sat up. She gathered her plate and empty can, then dragged herself to the kitchen, still half asleep. Draper made a brief appearance as if to remind her to fill the food dish before disappearing again. Maggie chuckled. She poured the dry food into the bowl and yelled out, "Happy now?" Of course the creature was nowhere in sight. Ambling off to bed, Maggie stretched and yawned. The bedside clock flashed neon blue numbers at her. Twelve eighteen. She'd fallen unconscious and slept almost two hours on the couch. It had been a good, deep sleep but not nearly long enough.

While brushing her teeth, Maggie wondered what Rayne was doing at this hour. Was she bent over her computer working on a paper? Analyzing results of experiments? Maybe she was pulling together information on Maggie's grant. The one she was eager to help write.

But as she completed her nightly ritual, the pictures changed from scientist to the sexy woman Maggie had watched come from her touch. It had been powerful and affirming for Maggie, but she wanted to know how it felt for Rayne. Sure, she'd proclaimed the standard OMG, but even the worst actress could fake it rather than hurt the other person's feelings. That's not what she wanted from Rayne. Had any of the women she'd slept with put on a show for her, knowing they would see each other at the gym and not wanting things between them to be awkward? Had Eve ever pretended to be satisfied with her? The thought was not only sobering, but worrisome. Would she have known if that had happened? She was in her early twenties back then. What did she know?

Maggie flopped into bed and snuggled beneath the covers. She was determined not to guess at the maybes of the past. The last thought she had before drifting off was one she had repeated like a mantra. Rayne would never be a casual lay.

CHAPTER THIRTY-TWO

The bed was piled with discarded clothes. Maggie had said to dress casually and comfortably, which gave her no clue at all. She'd tried to get more information, but Maggie was being tight-lipped, leaving her to fend for herself in the wardrobe department.

What did one wear to a casual, comfortable date? Should she eat something, or was dinner included? She tried not to anticipate the evening ending (maybe beginning) with sex, but she'd be kidding herself if there wasn't even a slim chance it would happen. After the sixth outfit, Rayne threw her hands in the air, deciding on simple and uncomplicated. Except there was lingerie to consider. Lace, silk, peekaboo, none at all. The garments wouldn't be seen if sex wasn't on the slate, so what did she care? More out of desperation than decision, Rayne pulled on a black camisole under a silky blue and black button-down shirt, along with dark jeans. She nodded at her reflection in the mirror before putting the finishing touches to her makeup, which she kept to a minimum. A spritz of her favorite perfume and out the door she went.

❖

"Shit!" Maggie said when Draper walked between her legs and got them both tangled up. In trying to avoid stepping on him, Maggie tripped over the damn animal and went crashing headlong into the dining room. She managed to avoid hitting her head, but her ankle had not fared as well. When she was able to roll over and sit up, she gave it a closer inspection, gingerly examining the area. Not broken, but definitely warm to the touch. She'd had experience with these type injuries since grade school, and she knew swelling wasn't far behind. She needed to get it wrapped and iced if she was going to be able to walk later.

Hobbling and holding on to furniture along the way got her to the bathroom. She had twenty minutes, give or take, before Rayne would arrive. She tended to run a little late, so she might catch a few extra minutes. If she hurried, she could wrap it and ice it for a few precious minutes. If the night ended with sex the jig would be up. She'd deal with it then. The best she could hope for was getting to their destination without drawing attention to her injury.

Maggie pulled and tugged to get the neoprene brace on her swelling ankle without too much pain. She wrapped the instant cold pack around it and secured it with the Velcro closure, then made it to the kitchen. The last thing she needed was the bottle of white wine and she put that in a special compartment of the rolling picnic basket she'd ordered from Amazon. Done for the moment, she sat in her recliner and elevated her foot. Draper came and sat on the floor in front of Maggie and looked up, his head tipped to one side.

"You are responsible for this." She pointed at her foot. "Nice going." Draper jumped up and sat on the arm of the chair, then cried for his dinner. "Ha! If you think I'm feeding you now, you're nuts," Maggie mumbled. Two minutes later, she pulled the pack off and stowed it in the freezer before the doorbell rang. She made it to the door without much of a limp, took a deep breath, and hoped their formal date, whatever that looked like, would go well. Rayne stood on the landing with her hands clasped in front of her, looking shy and adorable.

"Hi." She glanced behind Maggie's shoulder and waited. "Am I too early? I'm usually late, I know, but I was really trying to be on time for a change."

Rayne's rambling was cute, then she realized she was being rude. "You're right on time. Come on in." She stepped back carefully.

"Do you need help with anything? I hope this is okay." Rayne glanced down at her clothes. "You didn't give me much in the way of details so I wasn't sure if I should dress up or down, so I went somewhere in between."

Maggie shut the door and remembered at the last minute to pivot on her good foot. "You look great. Are you comfortable?" It was hard to tell with jeans, and the ones Rayne wore were form-fitting.

Rayne chuckled. "I learned a while ago to buy only jeans with spandex."

"Yeah, that's a game changer." She'd chosen a pair of darker jeans and a short-sleeved shirt, hoping it wasn't too casual. It was a stroke of luck that the weather had turned a little cooler and she could keep the ankle support out of view. Maggie clicked the remote on her car and grabbed the picnic basket. She walked a little slower and was mindful of how she stepped as she opened the door for Maggie. She lifted the basket into the car next to the thick blanket along with some cushions. She silently prayed she could walk to the picnic site. At least it wasn't her driving foot.

"Where are we going?"

Maggie pulled onto the road. "Not too far." It had taken a few hours and a lot of searching, but she'd found a babbling brook in the next town. It boasted some of the best views and classed it a "romantic destination on a warm summer evening." It wasn't technically evening yet, but she hoped it would still be beautiful. Ten minutes later, she parked on the side of the road. "I hope you don't mind a little walk."

"It's so pretty, I don't mind at all." Rayne met her at the back of the car. "Can I help?"

Maggie pulled a large reusable bag out and stuffed the blanket and cushions inside. "Would you mind carrying these?"

"Sure." Rayne slung the handles over her shoulder. "Lead the way."

It might have been easier to roll the basket, but the terrain was a bit bumpy, and it was more practical to carry it by the straps. By the time they reached the brook her foot was throbbing. She should take the brace off, but she didn't want Rayne to fuss over her. She also didn't want to take the chance it might swell up like a balloon if she did and she might not be able to get the brace on again. "Does this look like a good spot?"

"It's perfect." Rayne spread the blanket out, then placed the cushions next to each other at an angle. "What else can I do?"

Maggie hadn't been able to do much while she waited for Rayne to finish. Now that she was done, she had to get off her ankle, and she lowered herself carefully to the ground. "Let's have a drink before we eat and enjoy the scenery."

Rayne removed her shoes and socks, then plopped beside her. "Why don't you take yours off, too?"

Uh-oh. "Maybe in a bit." She got busy pulling out the wine carrier and two plastic wine glasses.

"How did you find this place?" Rayne asked as she took the offered glass.

"The internet is the modern-day version of a trail guide." She took a drink and hoped it would dull the throbbing. "The trick is knowing what keywords would give the best results."

"And you knew them?"

"Nope. I got lucky."

Rayne laughed. "You did well." Rayne's eyes sparkled. "So did I." She winked and spun around until she was lying with her head on the cushion, staring up at the billowy clouds that floated in front of a deep blue background. "I love looking at the sky." She turned and looked at her as she patted the space next to her. "You should give it a try."

As much as she wanted to enjoy the things Rayne was enjoying, the pain was distracting. The idea of trying to match Rayne's position wasn't appealing at all. Maybe it was time she confessed before Rayne thought she wasn't having a good time. "I'm sure it's a great view, but it's hard to move around a lot."

Rayne sat up. "What do you mean?"

"Draper and I got into a tumbling match, and I lost. I sprained my ankle in the process."

"Is that why you were walking so slow?" Rayne's eyes narrowed.

This date wasn't the time to lie or any way to strengthen a relationship. "Yes." She took a deep breath.

"We should go back. I'll take you to urgent care so you can have it x-rayed."

"This is not how our evening was supposed to go. Damn cat."

"Draper isn't responsible for your stubbornness." Rayne began gathering their things.

Maggie let her help her to her feet and the pain renewed, almost driving her to her knees. She gritted her teeth and pulled herself upright. Rayne stood in front of her, hands on her hips. "I'll be okay. I don't want to go to urgent care and sit for hours to find out it's a bad sprain when I already know that. Jill's working tonight. She knows how to wrap it properly so it will heal faster and give me stability." She must have given some clue that she wasn't going to budge. Rayne threw up her hands.

"Fine." She picked up the picnic duffel and handed her the bag. "I'm driving." When she opened her mouth to respond, Rayne spun on her with fire in her eyes. "Not. Another. Word."

The display of determination along with a good amount of spunk made her chuckle, but she kept the reaction inside. She didn't want to push her luck any further. Rayne wrapped her arm around her waist, and they began the slow trek to the car.

Rayne didn't say much on the ride to Maggie's house. When they walked into the gym, a woman came rushing up to them, her expression one of exaggerated concern. From the way she was acting, Rayne had the distinct impression the woman was familiar with invading Maggie's personal space, and she didn't like the idea of anyone getting that close to Maggie. She and Jill had politely steered the woman away from lavishing her attention on Maggie, but she'd been seething the whole time.

Jill had given Maggie a stern reprimand for being pig-headed, making her laugh. When they'd managed to get the brace off, the foot swelled. It was already a mottled display of purple. Jill wrapped the ankle and made Maggie promise she would ice it according to her directions.

When she opened the door, Draper sat on the rug, watching their every move. Once Maggie was settled, he sauntered over and sniffed at the bandage.

"This is all your fault, you little shit."

"Meow." Draper rubbed his head on Maggie's exposed toes, then jumped beside her.

Rayne shook her head as she rolled the bag into the kitchen. She grabbed an ice pack from the stack of them in the freezer, understanding for the first time why Maggie had so many. She wrapped it in a towel and draped it over the injury.

"Thank you. I feel terrible about ruining our night." Maggie looked sad. "I'm good now. You don't have to hang around."

How could Rayne be upset? Maggie had tried to ignore her pain in order not to disappoint Rayne. She clasped her hand over Maggie's and squeezed. "I'm staying. No need to struggle on your own." She went to the kitchen and rinsed the glasses they'd used, and grabbed the wine. "There's no sense letting a bottle of wine go to waste."

"I like the way you think."

She dug in her pocket and withdrew a small packet of pills. Jill had given them to her to be sure Maggie took them. She tore it open and dumped the contents into Maggie's empty hand. "Jill said to make sure you took them. Bottoms up."

Maggie looked from her hand to her wine. "With this?"

"Why not?"

Maggie rolled her eyes. "Can I please have water?"

"Gee, fine." She mumbled under her breath. She often took a handful of vitamins without much more than the spit in her mouth. "Here you go." After the pills were gone, she handed over the remote, careful not to jostle the couch when she sat. "I have no idea what was in the containers, but now that all the excitement has died down, I'm hungry." She glanced at Maggie who finally looked relaxed if not comfortable. "What about you?"

"I could eat, that's for sure." She finished her wine. "There are deluxe sandwiches from that little shop you like. Mixed fruit and yogurt. Some pickled veggies, and a bag of those really bad, but really good chips that we both moan over."

"We moan over more than chips."

Maggie groaned. "Injured person here."

"What if you don't have to move at all?" she asked. In her mind, she was working out the logistics of how they could both be satisfied without much movement on Maggie's part. It might be tricky, but she fully believed they could do it.

"I don't want to be a passive participant." Maggie cupped her chin and thumbed her cheek. "Not with you, Rayne."

How many women had she touched like that? Did the client, what was her name, reap the benefits of Maggie's talented hands in other ways? Was that why she fawned over Maggie when she saw her? It wasn't like she didn't know about the women Maggie slept with.

She told the voice to shut up. In spite of her own misgivings, Maggie's words reached her soul. To say she was falling for Maggie was an understatement. If she were being honest, she'd fallen for her so slowly throughout the time she'd known her it had taken until just recently to recognize the truth. "I'll get our food."

CHAPTER THIRTY-THREE

The smorgasbord was delightful. Rayne waited on her and cleaned up the remnants like many times before. During conversation lulls, Maggie tried to imagine what life with Rayne would look like. Would they have a genuine interest in their respective jobs and enjoy talking about their day, or were their professions so profoundly different there would be little or no discussion? Would Rayne be satisfied to stay where she was, or would she need to move to another institution, maybe even out of state, in order to advance her career? If Maggie got her wellness center off the ground and built a clientele would she pack it up and follow Rayne, wherever the science took her?

Maggie was getting way ahead of herself. They had only been dating a few weeks and she was already thinking about scenarios that might never happen. There were a lot of couples who managed to have meaningful relationships with vastly different jobs, and she was sure they would find time to indulge in shared interests. Rayne's offer to write a grant for startup money had to mean she was invested.

"You look exhausted. I should get going." Rayne fidgeted with a button on her shirt. "Do you want me to help you get to bed?"

"I appreciate the offer. I can manage for a night or two." She didn't want Rayne to leave. She wanted to be able to hold her and kiss her and hear her moan in pleasure. *Damn cat.* "Thank you for everything you did today."

"You would have done the same for me."

It was true, she probably would have, but what if she didn't have the same nurturing qualities? Was that something Rayne would want from their relationship? Maggie wasn't sure if she was valiant enough. "I'd try." She put her foot on the floor and pushed herself up, testing to see if her comfort level had changed over the last hour or so when she went to the bathroom.

"I can show myself out," Rayne said.

"You could, but I'm going to," Maggie said, sharper than she intended.

Rayne held up her hands in surrender. "Okay, okay. Gee, I only had your best interest at heart you know. No need to bite my head off."

"Sorry."

"I was pulling your uh…good leg."

The words made Maggie laugh. "You made a joke."

"Really though, how's the foot feeling?"

Maggie gingerly flexed it and was surprised at what little discomfort resulted from the movement. It was stiff, but not painful. "Not bad at all. I'm surprised it doesn't hurt as much as I expected it to."

"You have enough ice packs for the night. I've never seen so many."

"I put the used ones in storage bags and throw them in the freezer. You never know."

"You can take more OTC meds when you go to bed. Jill said every four to six hours."

"Are you okay? You look upset." She wasn't always good at reading people, but she'd tuned in to Rayne's emotions a while ago.

"Yes." Even though Rayne said she was fine, the vibes between them felt off.

"There's a pink elephant in the room that isn't going away just because we ignore it."

Rayne leaned against the door and looked at the floor for a long beat.

"Who was that?"

She wasn't about to lie. "Karen? The client at the gym tonight?"

Rayne's back stiffened. "Why does she have your number?"

It was Maggie's turn to stiffen. "Because I'm also her trainer. I gave it to you, too. Remember?"

"Vaguely."

The pissy attitude wasn't helping, especially since her foot was beginning to throb the longer she stood on it. "Why are you upset?"

Rayne shrugged. "She was overly friendly."

"You know I'm a personal trainer, and that I give my cell number to people."

"I know you give special attention to some of your clients." Rayne stood still studying her. "She was more concerned than a client would be. Did you sleep with her?"

"Lots of women act that way around me. You know that." Maggie hadn't hesitated, but she also didn't answer. Were they having their first argument?

"Is that a yes or a no?"

Maggie pursed her lips before she answered. "Yes, I slept with her once. Months ago."

"I didn't like her pawing at you." Rayne said with conviction.

"I wasn't keen about it either." Was Rayne really going to start an argument over someone Maggie fucked before they dated? Hell, before they'd even talked about it?

Rayne's face revealed a mix between sad and angry. This was not the way to celebrate going steady.

"I have to go." Rayne grabbed her keys and phone.

She took a minute to calm down. She was on the verge of making a rash decision she might regret. "Don't leave like this, Rayne. Let's talk about what's going on."

Rayne shook her head. "I don't think so." She reached for the doorknob. "Not tonight." Rayne kissed the corner of her mouth. "We'll talk tomorrow."

The door shut and Maggie stared at it. *What the hell just happened?* She limped to the couch. She replayed the scene at the gym. Rayne had her arm wrapped around her and Karen rushed over. Her hands *had* wandered a bit, but by that time she was in so much pain she hadn't been paying much attention. Then Jill took her other side and she had to practically shove Karen out of the way to help her to the recovery room. Had she said anything to Rayne? Maggie shook her head. Most of what happened was a blur.

Once she was in bed with a pillow under her foot, Maggie vowed to clear the air between them. Her reputation of being a player hadn't negatively affected her life, but she'd also not been serious about the women she slept with. Besides, it kept people at a distance and there hadn't been any plans to change her relationship status...until Rayne. Other women were diversions to her routine life and provided physical release. The night with Rayne had soothed her body and gave her grace to open herself to something more. Something deeper.

Maggie yawned and wished she could find a comfortable position. After ten minutes of moving and adjusting, she settled on her right side with the pillow supporting her foot. Thank goodness she remembered to take more medication. As it kicked in, she drifted, her last thoughts of Rayne and the warm glow of her smile.

❖

Avoidance wasn't a behavior Rayne engaged in often, but when she did, she went all out. She'd spent Sunday writing a draft of her next paper, then she'd effectively procrastinated over sending Maggie a text about how the previous night had ended on less than ideal terms. After accusing Maggie of the push you, pull me game, she felt guilty using it now and admitted it was exhausting.

She'd never been jealous of anyone, except for a few women she knew and admired for their ability to juggle a home life, work, and for most, children. That was a different type of jealousy. More like envy than anything. They were superheroes in her eyes. This feeling was far from that end of the spectrum. There was no reason to be so upset except for one common denominator, Maggie. How had her jealousy gotten out of hand so quickly? She needed to make amends and try to explain her irrational reaction to Maggie. But she was scheduled for a virtual meeting that started in ten minutes, then she was due to train a graduate student in a lab technique he had yet to master.

She typed off a quick message saying she hoped Maggie's ankle was better and that she'd call when she got home this evening. Everything would work out and Maggie would understand why she'd been upset. Maybe.

❖

Maggie looked at the clock for the dozenth time. Despite her assurance her ankle was on the mend, and she was capable of teaching classes, Jill had delegated her to desk duty for the next two days. She'd be bouncing off the walls by then.

Bad enough she hadn't heard from Rayne last night, and nothing today except for a quick text. She'd held out hopes for another message, but her phone had been silent. Karen hadn't called either, though that was a good thing. The day was dragging on and her anxiety grew with every passing moment. Maybe Rayne had invited her to bed to see what all the hoopla was about rather than a real desire to be with her. Now that she had, maybe Rayne hadn't enjoyed it as much as Maggie thought she had.

It hadn't felt that way at all, but then Maggie sometimes had a hard time evaluating a person's reactions. It all fell back to trusting her gut. She'd trusted it once and it ended in devastation. Not because of her poor choice or because there was any blame, but because there was no harbinger of what was to come. Last night, Rayne acted strange when she left, as though something more was bothering her. If so, she hadn't said anything, but still. Was Rayne's confusing demeanor an omen of what lay ahead? If so, what could she do to change the course, or did she even want to?

Life was so unpredictable. Just like people. The question remained—what did she want to do about Rayne since the ball was clearly in her court? Maggie glanced at the machines arranged on the gym floor as though they would provide an answer. Machines were orderly, predictable, and easy to recognize from their shape. About a third were occupied, and the rest of the clients were in classes. Jill had hired another fitness instructor. He seemed nice enough from the few minutes they had spoken. When it was just the three of them, days off and shorter workdays weren't much of an option. Everyone was looking forward to well-deserved opportunities of R and R. Would she have a chance to spend some of that time with Rayne?

She hadn't done anything wrong and that made Rayne's mood all the more confusing. Swallowing her pride and reaching out was an option. So was waiting for Rayne to come to her senses and admit something was off. To be honest, she didn't like either choice, but worrying wasn't going to provide resolution one way or another. "Fine," she mumbled to herself. If she didn't hear from Rayne by the time she got off, she would call. Not text, not email. She wanted to hear her voice. She also didn't want to give her an easy out. If she didn't pick up or call back, she'd have her answer.

CHAPTER THIRTY-FOUR

The paper was in draft mode sitting on Steve's desk. Rayne had also plotted out two experiments that would, hopefully, further prove her hypothesis. Science was so much fun. She did a little more research on the best organizations to submit the grant for Maggie's business startup and hoped she could come through on her promise to help her write a grant application that would be hard to ignore. All she needed was Maggie's outline and budget, but she worried Maggie might have changed her mind about accepting her help. The idea that Maggie knew she was upset about *something* wasn't a far stretch. If she couldn't tell her what was wrong, what did that say about their future?

She opened a bottle of flavored seltzer, filled a glass with ice, added half a shot of vodka, and added the bubbly water. She deserved it after working nonstop the last few days. *You mean nonstop avoidance of talking to Maggie.* She sighed. That too. She took a long drink before picking up her phone and studying the screen. The picture was of the waterfall she and Maggie had stumbled upon one of the first times they'd gone hiking.

Rayne was disappointed by her behavior. It wasn't good for her, and it certainly wasn't fair to Maggie. It's not like she'd called Karen or that Karen had pursued Maggie by staying around her despite Jill whisking Maggie away. Maybe Karen had called that night to check on Maggie's injury. She huffed. She didn't know Karen at all but that didn't change her feelings about Karen acting like she wanted to do more than console Maggie.

Did she really think Maggie would consider seeing another woman when she'd readily agreed to being exclusive? To the point she couldn't wait to take her on a formal date? Which was exactly what Rayne wanted. Had she already blown it with Maggie? She was scared that Maggie had decided to cut ties now, and avoid the heartache that might follow. After all, she told Rayne she was terrified of loving again if it brought more pain. Maybe that's why she hadn't contacted Rayne.

"I've lost a friend and my partner in one stupid act of unwarranted jealousy." *What the fuck was wrong with her?* She knew what she had to do. Swallow her pride and confess she acted out of jealous desperation. With her finger poised over Maggie's name, she took a breath. And then, the shrill ringtone scared the crap out of her. Maggie's face appeared and she fumbled the phone, sending it flying. It landed on the rug and slid under the chair. "Shit." Rayne dropped to the floor and reached all the way until she could grab it as it continued to make that insistent foghorn noise. She stabbed at the receiver icon, shouting, "Hello? Hello?" until the screen made the connection. She put it to her ear. "Hello?" If there was ever a good grief moment, this was it.

"Rayne?"

"Yes, I'm here." She was breathless and smiling.

"Are you okay?"

"I know it doesn't sound like it, but…it doesn't matter." She rolled her eyes. Impressive conversationalist she wasn't. At least not at the moment. *Get your shit together, Thomas.* "How's your ankle?"

"Better. Thanks." Maggie was quiet for a minute. "You haven't called, and I have no idea what that means."

She finished her drink for courage. "Because I'm a jerk."

"I'm sorry?"

"That's why I haven't called. I used every excuse I could find to not call because I'm a jerk."

Maggie laughed softly. "You aren't a jerk, but you are befuddling."

"I know. It's just…I didn't like it when Karen was all over you, and I know that wasn't your fault, but I couldn't help thinking she acted like she had a right to because you'd slept with her." Silence ensued. She checked her connection. Maggie was still there.

"You wouldn't be wrong."

"Oh."

"Yeah. It was only once because that's my MO. That's how I've always kept women at a distance. Karen seemed to think she'd be different, but she wasn't."

"Are we only once?"

"I don't know, are we?"

"If you're leaving it up to me, no, but I have to tell you I'm not going to be happy if there're others that think like Karen. I need exclusive, Mags." At least it was out in the open now.

"The last date was that good that now you want a picky promise? Sweet."

"Now who's being a jerk?"

"It's a trend," Maggie said.

Rayne snorted. Oh well, she couldn't take it back.

"Come over. Spend the night with me."

It was after eight. Not terribly late. "I have to work tomorrow."

"So do I."

"I'll have bed head in the morning." Rayne chewed her lip.

"I can't wait to tease you about it."

"Jerk."

"Yup. You'll have to come up with another pet name though. That one will never do."

"I'll be there in thirty minutes." What would she pack for her first sleepover?

"Why so long?" Sounds of Maggie moving around came through.

"Because I worked all day and I want to take a shower."

"Take one with me."

This was big. Showering together was intimate. Not that what they'd done last week wasn't, but this held the promise of a tighter bond. "Make that fifteen."

"I'll be ready."

Rayne raced through her house, throwing an ungodly and useless amount of stuff into a large tote. "It's one night." She made sure to include work clothes and at the last minute her toothbrush and toothpaste. She almost packed her hair dryer but talked herself down. She wasn't going to a foreign land. Maggie probably had a blow dryer. She slung her backpack over one shoulder, grabbed her keys, and hefted the tote. At the last minute she stared into the hallway mirror. "Don't fuck this up." If only she could be sure, she'd be a lot less nervous.

CHAPTER THIRTY-FIVE

Maggie laid out towels in the bathroom. She'd changed the sheets that morning, knowing she wouldn't feel like doing it when she got home. Bottles of water sat on the nightstands, and a few lit candles helped set the mood.

Yes, she had every intention of making love to Rayne. No, she didn't want a one and done with her. She'd thought from the beginning Rayne wasn't the type of woman who slept with another person easily. The bed was turned down, and the windows were open, allowing the soft warm breeze to carry the scent of peonies into the room. Maggie thought their perfume was intoxicating.

The doorbell rang and she couldn't help smiling. The misunderstanding between them had been just that. She asked questions and Rayne gave answers. She understood how easily words could lead to hurt feelings and insecurities. She was hoping for clarity between them from here on out and surprised herself by how easily the thought of seeing only Rayne settled her. This was what she wanted and needed. The others had only left her searching for something else.

"Hey," she said and opened the door wide. "Come in."

"Thanks." Rayne stared at her feet. Maggie reached for the tote bag she carried.

"Let me take that." The weight surprised her. "Are you moving in?"

Rayne's face fell. "I couldn't decide and then it just kept growing."

"Babe, I'm teasing." She brushed her lips over Rayne's soft, warm ones. One kiss would never be enough. Maggie carried the bag into her bedroom and returned to find Rayne still standing in the middle of the living room looking lost. She placed her hands on her arms. "Why are you so nervous?"

Rayne shook her head and finally looked up. "Because I almost messed this up once and I don't want to do it again." Unshed tears threatened to spill over.

"You didn't. Misunderstandings happen. Now we both know. We're good. Okay?"

"Okay." Rayne swiped her eyes.

"Can I get you something to drink?"

"I really need a shower."

"I happen to have one of those." Maggie kissed the top of Rayne's head and was happy to feel her relax a bit. She took her hand and led the way.

"Oh." Rayne did a small spin, taking in the space. "Which candle is that scent from?"

"It's from the peonies under the window. Do you like it?"

"It's wonderful."

They moved into the bathroom where Rayne stood again like a statue. Maggie loosened her pants, then pulled her shirt over her head. After she was naked, she stepped forward. "Will you let me undress you?"

Rayne took in a shuddery breath. "Yes." The word was barely audible, but Maggie heard her.

As they stood gazing at each other, Maggie couldn't stop her heart from soaring. Not that she wanted to. She'd done nothing but think about this scenario for more than two days. She'd been imagining the moment since meeting Rayne. There was something about her that captured her attention and sent her body into a near frenzy. *She's perfect and I'm going to show her.* When the water was ready, they stepped in together and Rayne sank against her.

"The water feels good, but you feel better." Rayne lifted her face, and Maggie obliged by wrapping her arms around her and then she took possession of her lips. Soft moans emanated from deep inside, and any doubts that lingered faded away before she gave them both a little room to breathe. "I want you more than I have wanted anything in my life." She turned Rayne until her back was nestled against Maggie's front. She covered her neck with kisses and slipped her hand between Rayne's thighs. Maggie entered her and found Rayne slick and ready. Her strokes were slow and deliberate. Rayne leaned further into her, and she pressed her back to the tiles warmed by the water. "Come for me?" She rubbed the hard knot, circling and pressing between strokes.

Rayne stiffened. "Feels so good." She grabbed her forearm and fiercely held on when her orgasm struck, gasping and whimpering.

Maggie held her tightly. "That's it, baby. Let go."

Several moments passed before Rayne turned. "Let's finish. I want to be lying next to you."

They made quick work of washing and rinsing, then dried with thick towels. Rayne climbed into bed and Maggie followed, pulling Rayne on top of her and lavishing her with kisses. Rayne reached between them, her fingers sliding through the wet heat.

"You feel amazing," Rayne said. "Soft and firm at the same time." Rayne circled her nipple with her tongue, and it tightened. "Can I go inside?"

"I wish you would." Maggie had a hard time getting out the words because everything Rayne did felt better than the touch before. Her excitement grew and Rayne responded by going deeper, stroking longer, driving her higher and higher until all she could do was feel and follow her touch. She guided Rayne's head until their mouths met, and she exploded. The fireworks on the inside of her eyelids momentarily blinded her.

"You're so damn sexy." Rayne kissed her softly and slowly withdrew.

"You bring out the beast in me." It was true. Rayne's touch was as magical as her tongue.

"Mmm. I like that I do." Rayne snuggled against her. "You feel like home."

No one had said those words to her. No one had ever made her feel like her love would be enough, not even Eve. "Rayne?"

"Hmm?" Rayne drew lazy circles on her chest.

"Would it be okay if I told you I love you?"

Rayne's fingers stopped moving and she rose to look at her. "You love me?"

Maggie nodded and held her breath, fearing it was too much, too soon. "It's okay if you don't feel the same." And it was. "I just wanted you to know."

Rayne's lips pressed together before she spoke. "Okay."

Maggie's heart sank.

Rayne kissed her passionately, deeply, fully. Then she settled on her chest again, leaving her to ponder if she'd been wrong in thinking Rayne's jealousy stemmed from a deeper desire.

"I love you, too."

Wait. What? She tipped Rayne's chin up to see her smiling. "Did you just say—"

"That's right. I love you."

Maggie was shocked, but not so shocked she couldn't respond. "Jerk."

"Yeah, I know." Rayne kissed her chest. "I really want to make love with you again, but I need a little recovery time." Rayne closed her eyes and sighed.

Maggie kissed the top of her head and pulled her closer. "Take all the time you want." She meant it. This love was new and different. They had so much to learn from and about each other. Maybe the way they'd fallen in love wasn't conventional, but it was real, and she was ready to explore the future with Rayne at her side. She couldn't predict where life would take them, but this was one experiment she believed they could see through together. If it didn't go as planned, that was okay, too, because Rayne knew how to get the results that would carry them for a long time. How could they fail when being in each other's arms felt like home for her, too?

About the Author

Renee Roman lives in upstate New York with her fur baby, Maisie. She is blessed by close friends, a loving partner, and a supportive family. She is passionate about many things including living an adventurous life, exploring her authentic self, and writing lesbian romance and erotica. Her book, *Escorted*, won the 2023 Golden Crown Literary Society Erotic Novel award.

You can find Renee on social media, her website, and online and in-person events. She enjoys interacting with readers via email at reneeromanwrites.com

Books Available from Bold Strokes Books

All This Time by Sage Donnell. Erin and Jodi share a complicated past, but a very different present. Will they ever be able to make a future together work? (978-1-63679-622-2)

Crossing Bridges by Chelsey Lynford. When a one-night stand between a snowboard instructor and a business executive becomes more, one has to overcome her past, while the other must let go of her planned future. (978-1-63679-646-8)

Dancing Toward Stardust by Julia Underwood. Age has nothing to do with becoming the person you were meant to be, taking a chance, and finding love. (978-1-63679-588-1)

Evacuation to Love by CA Popovich. As a hurricane rips through Florida, so too are Joanne and Shanna's lives upended. It'll take a force of nature to show them the love it takes to rebuild. (978-1-63679-493-8)

Lean in to Love by Catherine Lane. Will badly behaving celebrities, erotic sex tapes, and steamy scandals prevent Rory and Ellis from leaning in to love? (978-1-63679-582-9)

Searching for Someday by Renee Roman. For loner Rayne Thomas, her only goal for working out is to build her confidence, but Maggie Flanders has another idea, and neither are prepared for the outcome. (978-1-63679-568-3)

The Romance Lovers Book Club by MA Binfield and Toni Logan. After their book club reads a romance about an American tourist falling in love with an English princess, Harper and her best friend, Alice, book an impulsive trip to London hoping they'll each fall for the women of their dreams. (978-1-63679-501-0)

Truly Home by J.J. Hale. Ruth and Olivia discover home is more than a four-letter word. (978-1-63679-579-9)

View from the Top by Morgan Adams. When it comes to love, sometimes the higher you climb, the harder you fall. (978-1-63679-604-8)

Blood Rage by Ileandra Young. A stolen artifact, a family in the dark, an entire city on edge. Can SPEAR agent Danika Karson juggle all three over a weekend with the "in-laws," while an unknown, malevolent entity lies in wait upon her very skin? (978-1-63679-539-3)

Ghost Town by R.E. Ward. Blair Wyndon and Leif Henderson are set to prove ghosts exist when the mystery suddenly turns deadly. Someone or something else is in Masonville, and if they don't find a way to escape, they might never leave. (978-1-63679-523-2)

Good Christian Girls by Elizabeth Bradshaw. In this heartfelt coming of age lesbian romance, Lacey and Jo help each other untangle who they are from who everyone says they're supposed to be. (978-1-63679-555-3)

Guide Us Home by CF Frizzell and Jesse J. Thoma. When acquisition of an abandoned lighthouse pits ambitious competitors Nancy and Sam against each other, it takes a WWII tale of two brave women to make them see the light. (978-1-63679-533-1)

Lost Harbor by Kimberly Cooper Griffin. For Alice and Bridget's love to survive, they must find a way to reconcile the most important passions in their lives—devotion to the church and each other. (978-1-63679-463-1)

Never a Bridesmaid by Spencer Greene. As her sister's wedding gets closer, Jessica finds that her hatred for the maid of honor is a bit more complicated than she thought. Could it be something more than hatred? (978-1-63679-559-1)

The Rewind by Nicole Stiling. For police detective Cami Lyons and crime reporter Alicia Flynn, some choices break hearts. Others leave a body count. (978-1-63679-572-0)

Turning Point by Cathy Dunnell. When Asha and her former high school bully Jody struggle to deny their growing attraction, can they move forward without going back? (978-1-63679-549-2)

When Tomorrow Comes by D. Jackson Leigh. Teague Maxwell, convinced she will die before she turns 41, hires animal rescue owner Baye Cobb to rehome her extensive menagerie. (978-1-63679-557-7)

You Had Me at Merlot by Melissa Brayden. Leighton and Jamie have all the ingredients to turn their attraction into love, but it's a recipe for disaster. (978-1-63679-543-0)

All Things Beautiful by Alaina Erdell. Casey Norford only planned to learn to paint like her mentor, Leighton Vaughn, not sleep with her. (978-1-63679-479-2)

Appalachian Awakening by Nance Sparks. The more Amber's and Leslie's paths cross, the more this hike of a lifetime begins to look like a love of a lifetime. (978-1-63679-527-0)

Dreamer by Kris Bryant. When life seems to be too good to be true and love is within reach, Sawyer and Macey discover the truth about the town of Ladybug Junction, and the cold light of reality tests the hearts of these dreamers. (978-1-63679-378-8)

Eyes on Her by Eden Darry. When increasingly violent acts of sabotage threaten to derail the opening of her glamping business, Callie Pope is sure her ex, Jules, has something to do with it. But Jules is dead…isn't she? (978-1-63679-214-9)

Head Over Heelflip by Sander Santiago. To secure the biggest prizes at the Colorado Amateur Street Sports Tour, Thomas Jefferson will do almost anything, even marrying his best friend and crush—Arturo "Uno" Ortiz. (978-1-63679-489-1)

Letters from Sarah by Joy Argento. A simple mistake brought them together, but Sarah must release past love to create a future with Lindsey she never dreamed possible. (978-1-63679-509-6)

Lost in the Wild by Kadyan. When their plane crash-lands, Allison and Mike face hunger, cold, a terrifying encounter with a bear, and feelings for each other neither expects. (978-1-63679-545-4)

Not Just Friends by Jordan Meadows. A tragedy leaves Jen struggling to figure out who she is and what is important to her. (978-1-63679-517-1)

Of Auras and Shadows by Jennifer Karter. Eryn and Rina's unexpected love may be exactly what the Community needs to heal the rot that comes not from the fetid Dark Lands that surround the Community but from within. (978-1-63679-541-6)

The Secret Duchess by Jane Walsh. A determined widow defies a duke and falls in love with a fashionable spinster in a fight for her rightful home. (978-1-63679-519-5)

Winter's Spell by Ursula Klein. When former college roommates reunite at a wedding in Provincetown, sparks fly, but can they find true love when evil sirens and trickster mermaids get in the way? (978-1-63679-503-4)

Coasting and Crashing by Ana Hartnett Reichardt. Life comes easy to Emma Wilson until Lake Palmer shows up at Alder University and derails her every plan. (978-1-63679-511-9)

Every Beat of Her Heart by KC Richardson. Piper and Gillian have their own fears about falling in love, but will they be able to overcome those feelings once they learn each other's secrets? (978-1-63679-515-7)

Grave Consequences by Sandra Barret. A decade after necromancy became licensed and legalized, can Tamar and Maddy overcome the lingering prejudice against their kind and their growing attraction to each other to uncover a plot that threatens both their lives? (978-1-63679-467-9)

Haunted by Myth by Barbara Ann Wright. When ghost-hunter Chloe seeks an answer to the current spectral epidemic, all clues point to one very famous face: Helen of Troy, whose motives are more complicated than history suggests and whose charms few can resist. (978-1-63679-461-7)

Invisible by Anna Larner. When medical school dropout Phoebe Frink falls for the shy costume shop assistant Violet Unwin, everything about their love feels certain, but can the same be said about their future? (978-1-63679-469-3)

Like They Do in the Movies by Nan Campbell. Celebrity gossip writer Fran Underhill becomes Chelsea Cartwright's personal assistant with the aim of taking the popular actress down, but neither of them anticipates the clash of their attraction. (978-1-63679-525-6)

Limelight by Gun Brooke. Liberty Bell and Palmer Elliston loathe each other. They clash every week on the hottest new TV show, until Liberty starts to sing and the impossible happens. (978-1-63679-192-0)

Playing with Matches by Georgia Beers. To help save Cori's store and help Liz survive her ex's wedding they strike a deal: a fake relationship, but just for one week. There's no way this will turn into the real deal. (978-1-63679-507-2)

The Memories of Marlie Rose by Morgan Lee Miller. Broadway legend Marlie Rose undergoes a procedure to erase all of her unwanted memories, but as she starts regretting her decision, she discovers that the only person who could help is the love she's trying to forget. (978-1-63679-347-4)

The Murders at Sugar Mill Farm by Ronica Black. A serial killer is on the loose in southern Louisiana and it's up to three women to solve the case while carefully dancing around feelings for each other. (978-1-63679-455-6)

Fire in the Sky by Radclyffe and Julie Cannon. Two women from different worlds have nothing in common and every reason to wish they'd never met—except for the attraction neither can deny. (978-1-63679-573-7)